DON'T FALL FOR THE FAKE BOYFRIEND

A SWEET ROMCOM

LACEY BOLT

SECOND TURN PUBLISHING, LLC

LEARN MORE

Want to know when Lacey's next book is coming out? Want to get free content and know when discounts happen? Just curious as to what Lacey is doing? Then sign up for her newsletter at laceybolt.com/fake_boyfriend!

EMILY

The quiet murmur of patients and staff walking down the hospital corridor outside of Emily's social work office was interrupted by a jolting knock on Emily's office door. She looked up in time to see the nurse who recently transferred to work in the hospice unit. Emily pasted on a smile and tried to look like Theresa hadn't interrupted her in the middle of a crisis. She shuffled a few papers on her desk to cover the wedding invitation.

Theresa stomped into Emily's office and collapsed on the chair opposite her desk. "Mr. Palmer's wife called again. She's freaking out because he isn't hungry. Can you call her back? I'm tired of dealing with her."

Emily tried to hide her frown. She'd been a social worker in the hospital for the past five years, and worked in the hospice unit for four of those five years. The Palmers were the definition of easy hospice patients. "I'll call her. She is sweet. You should ask her about her quilting hobby. She's made some really nice quilts and donates the small ones to the pediatric oncology unit. I'm sure she'd love to show you some next time you stop by their house to check on Mr. Palmer."

"I'm not interested in quilting. Besides, she doesn't like me. She only calls me to complain about things. I keep telling her to call you instead, since you're the social worker, but she ignores me." Theresa spoke to her nails, barely sparing a look in Emily's direction.

Emily considered her words carefully. "She is scared of losing her husband. She just needs some reassurance that she's not alone."

"We've been at her house twice in the past week. How could she possibly feel alone?"

Emily pursed her lips. Maybe Theresa had never lost someone she loved or even gone through a bad breakup. Maybe she'd never felt the stabbing pain in her heart when the person she thought would stand by her side for the rest of her life looked her in the eye and said he was in love with her cousin. Maybe she didn't feel the loneliness seep into her bones as she packed up her belongings, wondering if he had been thinking about her cousin instead of her when they painted the walls in the living room or picked out the items for their wedding registry.

"How about we go visit her together tomorrow? I have a list of patients to see at the Sunnyvale nursing home in the morning. We could start the day there, go see Mrs. Palmer, and then see a few more patients later in the afternoon," Emily said. They both worked for the hospice department in the hospital, so it made sense to visit some of their shared patients together. Since Theresa was a nurse and Emily was a social worker, both of them should be able to work together to help their patients.

Theresa chewed her lip and then nodded. "Sure. Maybe if we go together, the patients won't hate me as much."

"They don't hate you." Hate was the feeling you got when an ivory envelope came in the mail containing the invitation for your cousin's wedding—with your ex-fiancé.

"They definitely don't like me." Theresa exhaled dramatically. "Whatever. I don't really care if they like me or not. But it would be easier if we carpooled tomorrow. Meet you here at nine?"

Emily nodded and Theresa rose from the chair. "See you then." Emily glanced at her desk and saw the sheet of paper with the list of men's names written on it. She grimaced. "Hey, Theresa?"

Theresa turned around, hand on the doorknob. "Yeah?"

"Um, I was wondering, well . . . do you have any guy friends who. . . ugh, never mind. Forget I said anything."

Theresa stared at her with a sly smile. "Are you looking for a date?"

"No, I shouldn't have asked. I'm just trying to find a date for this, um, event that I need to attend. Just don't want to go alone." She shrugged, trying to look as though it wasn't important and that the thought of going to the wedding alone hadn't kept her awake each night for the past week.

"Why would you have trouble getting a date? You're attractive."

Emily tried not to cringe. Her brown shoulder-length hair was unremarkable, at least that's what her ex-fiancé had said. And her matching brown eyes were the color of mud, as he once not-so-kindly stated.

"When is this event?" Theresa asked.

"Next Saturday."

"I could ask my neighbor, but he usually works weekends."

Emily considered her offer. Was she really desperate enough to have a blind date with a stranger? He could be a serial killer . . . or have bad breath. "Don't worry about it. I'll figure something out."

"Alright. See you tomorrow." With a small wave, Theresa left the office.

Emily picked up a pen and examined the list of potential dates for the wedding. She crossed off the name of her new neighbor, Kurt. No one in her family would believe she was dating a smoker. What about Ivan? His office was just two doors down the hallway from hers. He never smoked. He annoyed her most of the time, they disagreed on almost everything, and he acted like he was the only social worker in their department who deserved the job title. Maybe she could tolerate him for one day?

She crossed off his name and the next two names on the list.

She should fake a car accident. Or appendicitis. Skip the entire wedding. Her mother would probably disown her, and her aunts would bring up her failed relationship at every single family gathering, but she could handle that.

It couldn't be any worse than when her great-uncle didn't hold the door open for her grandmother at a charity event in the 1970s. That incident still made its way into her grandmother's annual Christmas letter. Her grandmother wouldn't possibly describe her absence at this wedding in this year's letter, right?

She had to go.

There had to be someone she hadn't thought of yet. She picked up her phone and tapped until a list of her contacts appeared.

Adam, the handyman at her apartment, was old enough to be her grandfather. Alan was closer to her age but married. Bennet gave her the chills—in all the wrong ways.

She kept scrolling through her phone. There weren't really any options there.

A new guy made her drink at the coffee shop this morning. Would it be completely awkward to approach him tomorrow morning? *Hello, I'd like to order a tall mocha latte and invite you to attend a wedding as my guest and fake boyfriend. Formal attire, please, and the reception will be on a boat. I promise that I'll be a horrible date since I cannot even look at a boat without getting sick. Oh, and what's your name?*

Emily grabbed her phone. Desperate times required desperate phone calls. She called her best friend and cousin, Ashley.

Ashley picked up on the second ring.

"Ash, I can't find a date for the wedding, and it's a week from tomorrow."

"Does this mean what I think it means?" Ashley's voice rose an octave as she spoke.

"Yes."

Ashley started squealing. Emily held the phone away from her ear until the noise decreased.

"I know exactly who I'm going to set you up with. I've been dying to get the two of you on a date together! I'll call him and see if he's free tonight. Michael and I were going to grab dinner together. If he's free, we can go on a double date!"

Ashley's excitement was undeniable but not contagious. Ever since she had been in a relationship with her cardiologist boyfriend, Michael, she had tried to set Emily up with his best friend and fellow cardiologist, Bill. Ashley didn't know that Emily asked Bill out on a date a few months ago. Either Bill didn't hear her, or he pretended that he didn't hear her. They saw each other a few times since then, always surrounded by other people, and he never showed any more interest in her. She wasn't going to set herself up for more rejection.

Emily needed to put some brakes on Ashley's excitement. "Sure. But not Bill. I'll meet anyone except him."

Ashley was silent. Emily glanced at her phone's screen to make sure the call hadn't disconnected.

"Ash?"

"I'm here. And I'm really excited that you are going to start dating again—"

"I'm not dating. I just need a fake date for the wedding so I don't humiliate myself."

Ashely tried again. "I don't know what you have against Bill—"

"He's a playboy and you know it."

Silence hung in the air for a few seconds. Ashley didn't deny the accusation.

"You must know someone else who would go with me."

"Bill used to be a player but Michael says he's a great guy. He's changed." Michael and Ashley had been dating for the past four months, after a rocky start to their relationship. Michael was a hot-shot cardiologist, one of the best in the region, and Ashley mopped up the hospital floors. Their story wasn't exactly a modern-day Cinderella, but it made Emily start to think that there was hope for her again.

"I don't believe in people changing. Once a player, always a player. How long has Michael known Bill?" And how many skeletons were in his closet?

"They met in medical school, I think."

"Has he ever been engaged?" Or cheated on anyone?

"Emily, stop looking for excuses to avoid him."

Emily resisted the urge to roll her eyes. "All I'm saying is that, since you've started dating Michael, I've hung out with you two and Bill a few times. He's never brought a date. But remember that fundraiser last month? He danced with nearly every woman there and I swear I saw at least three women give him their phone numbers."

"What's that supposed to mean?"

Emily let out a long sigh. "It means that he can't make a commitment. When was his last long-term relationship?"

"You aren't looking for a long-term relationship. Just someone to go with you to the wedding."

"I'm not going to ask him to go to the wedding." Emily squeezed her eyes shut. "There must be someone else you can set me up with. Someone who doesn't flirt with every available woman. Someone who is capable of making a long-term commitment without constantly waiting for the next opportunity to cheat."

"First, I don't think he's the type of guy to have one-night stands. Second, he's not like Ethan." Ashley's words came out quietly and slowly.

Emily flinched as she realized how harsh her words were. "I know that."

"Do you?" Doubt dripped off of Ashley's voice. "Ethan treated you like trash, but not all guys are like that. You have to take a risk on another guy if you don't want to be alone forever."

"I'm not looking for someone to be with forever. I just need a date for this weekend. And I don't want to bring someone who's going to collect phone numbers like it's their hobby and leave the reception with another woman."

"Michael said that Bill's never cheated on anyone."

Unlike Ethan.

Emily chewed on her lip as she considered her choices. There really were no other options at this point, except to go to the wedding alone.

Ashley took advantage of the silence. "This is the perfect weekend for you to start dating again. And it won't even be a real date, right? So there's really no risk. You have to get back in the game at some point."

"This entire thing is a bad idea. I should just skip the wedding."

"If you only need a fake date, he's perfect. He's hotter than Ethan, more successful than Ethan, and no one will feel any pity for you after they see you with him. Plus, I heard that he's an amazing dancer."

Emily snorted. "I doubt I'll be able to do any dancing on the trip. I'll probably be stuck to the side of the boat, trying not to get sick."

"If you don't want to go with Bill, I don't have any other ideas for dates. No one at my restaurant would be a good choice. Most of the guys are dating or married, and anyway, they all work on Saturday."

Emily pictured the contents of her grandmother's upcoming Christmas letter. "Fine. I guess Bill is my best option."

"He's an amazing option, Emily. We'll all hang out tonight and you'll have fun, I promise."

"I wish you were going to the wedding too, Ash. I could really use the support."

Ashley made a soft noise. "You know I wasn't invited. Veronica is your cousin, not mine."

"I know." It was true. Ashley's mother and Emily's father were siblings. Veronica was her cousin on Emily's mom's side of the family. There was little interaction between the two sides of her family.

"I'll make plans for tonight and text you later with the details. I'm sure Bill won't say no to taking you to the wedding. Besides, he owes Michael and me a favor."

Emily picked up a pen and started stabbing a piece of paper on her desk. If Bill needed coercion to date her, then she wasn't sure she wanted to take him. Except that he really was gorgeous, in an underwear-model type of way. And he would definitely turn heads at the wedding, which was exactly what she needed if she wanted to avoid constant looks of pity from everyone who knew her history.

She hated to admit it, but Bill would be the perfect date for this wedding. As long as he agreed, put his playboy tendencies on hold, and promised not to flirt with any other woman during their fake date.

2

EMILY

Emily tapped her fingers on the table in the restaurant. Of course, she was the first one there. Ashley texted just a few minutes ago to let her know that she and her boyfriend, Michael, were stuck in traffic. There was no way to know if Bill was still coming. Why would he agree to meet up for a double date, anyway? Unless Ashley and Michael didn't tell him that it was a double date. Or maybe he thought it was a double date between Ashley, Michael, and whomever Bill was dating at the moment. Would he show up with his own date? She couldn't ask him to go to the wedding in front of another woman. That would be the definition of mortifying.

No, wait, the definition of mortifying would be showing up at your ex-fiancé's wedding without a date.

She could just leave right now. Go back to her car, spy on the entrance to the restaurant, and wait until Ashley, Michael, and Bill arrived. If Bill arrived with some gorgeous model, she could drive away and not look back.

Unless Bill and his potential date arrived separately and met inside, at the table, then she'd be the awkward, single person in a group of couples.

The miserable fifth wheel.

She checked the time again as the server came by to refill her water glass and considered her other options. She couldn't leave the table without leaving a tip, at the very least. She had four dollars in her wallet. She doubted that would be enough to convince the server to pretend that she'd never been there.

No, the only option was to face the music. She'd had a momentary lack of judgment when she thought about begging Bill to be her fake date. There was no reason for her to follow through on the plan. She could find an excuse to miss the wedding. For instance, she could tell everyone that her dog ate a shoe and needed emergency surgery at the vet. She probably had time to adopt a dog before the wedding.

She groaned and rested her head in her hands, closing her eyes.

Just a few seconds later, a subtle cough drew her attention.

A gorgeous man stood next to the table, hand on the back of the chair nearest to her. He must have grown since she saw him last. He was easily a few inches over six feet tall with large, muscular arms that stretched the sleeves of his button-up shirt. His dark, wavy hair was combed back neatly, as if he hadn't spent the majority of the day walking the halls of a hospital. She refused to look at his lower half. If she remembered correctly, he was a cardiologist at a different hospital in the city. None of the doctors in her own hospital looked remotely like him. The doctor in charge of the hospice unit was old and wrinkled. Bill was definitely not.

He raised his eyebrows in question and tentatively pulled out the chair at the table. "Emily?"

She nodded, trying to hide the sour taste in her mouth. "Guilty. Ashley and Michael are running late." Seriously, they had met at least five times over the past few months. Once before Ashley and Michael started dating, at a bar after Ashley and Michael realized they were practically meant for each other, and at a few different social gatherings. Plus, she had a short conversation with him at the hospital fundraiser, the same night he collected at least three phone numbers from other women.

He sat down and caught the attention of the server. The woman walked over to the table, and Bill flashed her a large grin with his perfect teeth, and, yes, there was one dimple. Predictably, the server started to blush.

Emily didn't even listen to what he said to the waitress. She wouldn't be surprised if the server gave her phone number to him by the end of the night. She could never compete with that, and she didn't want to try. If her relationship with her lying and cheating fiancé had taught her anything, it was that good-looking men couldn't be trusted. And while Ethan was definitely attractive, he looked like yesterday's leftovers compared to Bill.

Emily grabbed her phone and sent Ashley another text. *Where are you?!?!* She had just hit the Send button when Bill thumped a menu in front of her. She looked up to see both him and the waitress staring at her expectantly.

"Sorry, just sending a text. Did you need something?"

Bill motioned to the menu. "I'm starving and want to order an appetizer for the table. I don't think Michael and Ashley will care if we start without them. What do you like?"

She scanned over the menu quickly. Most of the appetizers looked good. "How about the spinach and cheese dip?" As soon as she said the words, she regretted it, picturing how she'd look with bits of spinach stuck in her teeth. "Wait, no, how about . . ." she scanned the other items quickly and picked one randomly. "Shrimp cocktail?" Again, bad choice. Shrimp made her gag.

He turned to the waitress. "We'll take the shrimp and the

spinach dip, please." He turned back to Emily. "I'm allergic to shrimp," he said in explanation.

The waitress walked away, leaving the two of them alone. They sat in awkward silence for a few seconds until Emily's phone dinged. She looked at it and held it out for Bill to see.

"Ash says they are stuck in traffic. It'll be a few more minutes before they get here."

He didn't look happy at the news. He looked around the restaurant, scanning over the crowd.

That reminded Emily of something. "Are you expecting someone else tonight? Do we need another chair at the table?" *For your date?* She wanted to add the last part but couldn't.

He faced her and scratched his neck, looking confused. "No, I think it's just the four of us tonight."

"Oh, right."

"Did you think someone else was coming?" He started looking around the restaurant again.

"No, I was just wondering because you were looking around the restaurant."

He brought his gaze back to her again. "Is it a crime to look around a room?"

Emily frowned. "No, it's just—oh, never mind. Forget that I said anything."

He didn't speak again. So much for good conversation. If they couldn't even converse for five minutes alone, how would she possibly survive the long car ride, ceremony, and reception? No one would think they were actually dating if they couldn't string together more than two sentences at a time.

She tried again. "It is a really pretty restaurant, isn't it? I heard that the building used to be a factory, which is why they left the ceiling exposed."

He stopped scanning the room again and returned his

gaze to her. She pointed to the ceiling. "It does kind of look like it could have been a factory a long time ago, right?"

He looked up and studied the ceiling briefly. "I guess so." He looked back at her. "So, Michael said that you need a favor?"

Ugh. He went right to the point. Ashley must have told Michael, who told Bill. She wondered how much he knew. And if it was too late to back out.

She picked up her menu again and pretended to scan over the main entrees. "No, not really. I mean, I thought I needed help with something, but not anymore. Problem solved." She tried to look nonchalant. She peeked a quick look at him out of the corner of her eyes.

His eyes were locked on someone. One quick glance in the direction of her gaze confirmed her suspicion. Two female servers stood at a table across the room, talking to a customer by the back door. One had long, naturally blond hair, while the other's hair was dark at top and gradually turned blond toward the ends. Both wore the server uniforms like the clothing had been custom-tailored for their bodies.

Emily looked down at her own clothing. She'd changed into a black skirt and navy shirt after work, and had tried to ignore how the skirt felt tighter than it did the last time she wore it, thanks to the extra servings of late-night ice cream since receiving the wedding invitation. Some of Ethan's last words floated into her mind as one of the two women gracefully stepped back from the table. He had come home hours late, again, claiming that he had to work overtime. She now knew that he'd come back from a date with another woman, but didn't know it back then.

She had walked out of the kitchen to greet him by the front door of their apartment. "I heated up dinner. It's on the table. I made your favorite, lasagna, and a salad."

Ethan barely shrugged his shoulders before walking across the apartment towards the bedroom. "I'm not hungry."

"I waited to eat until you came home." Not to mention that it took her over an hour to make his favorite meal.

He turned toward her and she saw a glimmer of hope wash over her as he looked at her intently, with something almost like concern filling his eyes. "You should just eat the salad. And go to the gym instead of wasting your time making lasagna. Don't you care about looking good for me? Or maybe do something with your hair." Ethan turned his back on her and walked into their bedroom. The sound of the shower running filled the apartment as she walked into the kitchen and stared at the lasagna, oozing with melted cheese and sauce.

She still regretted not ending their relationship that night. She should have known better. She shouldn't have been so blindsided the next day when she learned the truth. That he'd been cheating.

And she should have grown thick enough skin that all his comments about her looks didn't make her feel as insecure as she felt right now, watching someone as handsome as Bill stare at the servers across the room at the restaurant.

No man was ever going to make her feel the same way Ethan made her feel.

She slammed her menu down on the table in front of her, drawing his attention. "Seriously, we've been sitting here for less than five minutes together, and you can't even act like you want to be here? Don't pretend that you aren't looking around the room again. My eyes work very well, and it's very clear that you are looking for someone more interesting than me. Go ahead and ask the waitress for her number when she comes back. I don't care. In fact, I really should be leaving."

She stood up before Bill had a chance to say anything and

promptly ran into Ashley, who had just walked up to the table with Michael.

"Em!" Ashley gave Emily a big hug, either unaware or pretending to be unaware that Emily just snapped at Bill. "So sorry we're late."

Michael gave her a brief hug as well and then sat down at the table. Emily stood awkwardly next to her chair. Bill refused to look at her.

"Em?" Ashley tilted her head at Emily and motioned to the chair. Emily frowned and sat back down on the hard chair. She'd already created one scene; she did not want to create another.

The waitress chose that moment to bring the appetizers to the table. Emily glanced at Bill out of the corner of her eye and saw him staring pointedly at her.

She returned his gaze directly, then tilted her head towards the waitress and raised her eyebrows, silently daring him to get her number now that their friends had joined the table.

He deliberately crossed his arms, leaned back in his chair, and shook his head subtly, all while refusing to break eye contact with Emily.

She broke the eye contact first, only to notice that Ashley had watched their entire interaction. *Bathroom?* Emily silently mouthed the word to Ashley and raised her eyebrows.

What? Ashley mouthed back.

Bathroom? Emily mouthed the words more carefully and then looked around the room. There were no signs for the ladies' room, and she had no idea where it was, so she couldn't point in the direction. But really, how hard could it be for someone to lip-read 'bathroom'?

BATHROOM! Emily tried one last time but was met with a shrug from Ashley. She frowned.

Before she could come up with another plan to get Ashley away from the table, Bill placed three pieces of shrimp on her plate. Emily stared at the pale lumps of slimy seafood. Was that some type of disgusting piece offering?

Emily tried not to gag from the stench. "Thanks," she mumbled without looking at Bill.

"Aw, Bill, you are so sweet. But Emily hates shrimp." Ashley picked up her own empty plate and held it out to Emily. "I'll trade with you, Em."

Emily didn't look at Bill as she swapped her shrimp-laden plate with Ashley's empty plate. She reached for the spoon in the spinach dip and placed some on her plate, along with a handful of chips that came with the dip. She took a large bite. It was so good.

She finally glanced at Bill, expecting him to be staring at the waitress or another attractive female again. Instead, he was staring at her.

She shrugged and took another bite of spinach dip.

"So, what was the big favor that Emily needed from you?" Michael asked Bill while snatching a piece of shrimp off Ashley's plate.

Emily froze, mid-chew.

Bill leaned back in his chair. "She hasn't asked me yet. But I'm dying to know." His words were laced with something, either sarcasm or mockery.

Everyone looked at her now. She pointed to her mouth and started chewing again, covering her mouth with her hand. If she took long enough, maybe they would start talking about something else. But they all stared silently.

Ashley gave her a subtle, encouraging nod. Michael looked curious. But Bill . . . he looked like he enjoyed her discomfort.

She quickly ran her tongue over her teeth and didn't feel

any spinach stuck there. But just to be safe, she took a quick sip of water.

They were all still staring.

She sighed. "It's nothing. I thought I needed help with something, but it turns out that I don't need anything after all."

Ashley gasped. "You found a date for the wedding? Who?"

Michael turned to Ashley. "That was the favor? She needed a date for a wedding?"

"Yup." Ashley nodded.

"Why couldn't you just go alone?" Bill asked.

Emily shrugged. "Do you all know what you want to order? I'm thinking of getting the pasta."

"She can't go alone to the wedding because it's her ex-fiancé's wedding," Ashley explained.

"Why would anyone go to their ex-fiancé's wedding?" Bill didn't bother to mask the disgust in his voice.

"She has to go. He's marrying her cousin."

"Aren't you going too, Ashley?" Bill asked.

"Nope. Wrong side of the family. My mom and Emily's dad are siblings. This cousin is on Emily's mom's side of the family. I'm not related and I wasn't invited."

"Doesn't Emily have any siblings who will be at the wedding? She can hang out with them."

Emily closed her eyes and tried to pretend that Bill and Ashley weren't having a conversation about her, as if she wasn't seated next to them.

"Emily's an only child," Ashley said. "Half of the guests at the reception will be from Ethan's family. Emily invited them to her own wedding, before it was cancelled. The other guests will be Veronica's relatives. Again, most of them were invited to Emily's wedding."

"She can skip it."

"She can't. Her mother will kill her."

"Then why can't she go alone?"

"If she goes alone, everyone at the wedding will gossip about her."

Bill shook his head. "I don't get it. People break off engagements all the time. It sucks that he's marrying her cousin, but stranger things happen."

Emily dropped her menu on the table with a thud. "This is my problem, and I'll fix it myself. I don't need anyone's help or anyone's pity. If you really need to know"—she turned and pointed at Bill—"I was going to ask you to go with me to the wedding because *everyone* in my family knows that she started dating him over a year ago, but I only found out about it four months ago when he broke off our engagement. So yes, the cheating pig who broke my heart is getting married next Saturday, and I can't get out of going to their wedding. But, like I said, it's my problem, and I'll handle it myself."

The table was silent. Emily pulled her hands to her lap and tried to stop shaking.

"The wedding is next Saturday?" Bill's voice was quiet as he spoke, without any trace of jeer.

She nodded and stood up. "I'm heading home. Sorry, Ashley, I had a long day. I'll call you tomorrow."

She walked away from the table without looking back. Hopefully, Ashley and Michael wouldn't be mad at her tomorrow.

She reached the front of the restaurant and paused at the hostess desk, coat ticket in hand. The front hostess was nowhere in sight. As she scanned the entryway for anyone who could help retrieve her jacket, she saw Bill walking in her direction.

She turned away from him and realized, too late, that her nose was an inch away from the wall. She turned back awkwardly.

Bill leaned casually against the wall. He looked straight ahead instead of at her. When he spoke, she wasn't entirely sure he was talking to her. But there was no one else around.

"The food here is overpriced. But I'm still hungry. How about we ditch Ashley and Michael and head down the street to another place?"

Her stomach growled at the mention of more food. She glanced around for the hostess again. If it weren't raining outside, she would have just left without her jacket. "I don't need anyone's pity. I'm going home."

"I'm not asking out of pity."

"I don't believe you."

He let out a heavy sigh and turned to her. "I'm hungry. I don't want to be a third wheel to Ashley and Michael. I wouldn't be a third wheel if you stayed at the table. But you left. So now I'm leaving. I'm still hungry, and I hate eating alone."

Emily's heart sank. If Ashley were standing next to her, Ashley would remind her that it wasn't her responsibility to help everyone she saw. But Ashley wasn't there.

"Fine. I'll go with you."

3

EMILY

Bill's choice of a good restaurant was questionable, at best. The dining area was small, with tiny tables placed close together. As soon as Emily and Bill walked in, he directed her to one of those small tables in the back corner. He politely pulled out a seat for her before settling in the opposite chair with his back against the wall.

Chivalry wasn't dead after all.

Emily glanced at the menu in front of her before looking up at him. "What's good to eat here?" She bit her tongue and didn't say what she was actually thinking. Hopefully, he wouldn't recommend anything that would give her food poisoning.

That is, if he would stop looking around the room long enough to engage in conversation.

She cleared her throat loudly. He looked at her expectantly. "Do you have any recommendations? I haven't been here before."

He slowly drew up the corners of his mouth in a smirky grin. "I heard that the shrimp linguine is a customer favorite."

She frowned. "Ok, fine. I'll pick out something on my own."

"The mushroom ravioli is my favorite."

That surprised her. "Really? I thought you'd be more of a steak and potatoes type of guy."

He shook his head. "The guy who owns this place would kick you out in a heartbeat if he heard you speak like that."

"So you know the owner?"

"I've met him. His son runs the place now. He and I are good buddies. If he's here tonight, he'll come out to say hello."

"Hmm." Emily looked at the menu again. She wished she'd had the guts to go home instead of following him here like a lost puppy dog. If she ordered quickly, maybe she could be finished and back home within the hour. Or she could fake an emergency.

She couldn't pretend that Ashley was calling her, because they just left her and Michael at the last restaurant. A work emergency could be believable. But that meant she'd have to lie. She hated lying with a passion.

And yet, here she was, stuck at a restaurant with a ladies' man because she had a moment of weakness and was now actually considering lying to her entire family and pretending that he was her date to the wedding.

Bill waited until she put down her menu to speak. "So, about the wedding . . ."

She looked at him critically. He was no longer looking around the restaurant but focused on her with his arms crossed. She couldn't tell if he wanted to see her squirm or liked poking at people's wounds.

She squared her shoulders and sat up straight. "I meant what I said at the last restaurant. I can handle my own problems."

"I'm sure you can."

"I can." Emily pressed her lips together tightly.

He narrowed his gaze. "What I can't figure out is why you don't have a boyfriend who will go with you."

Emily tried to suppress a groan. "Right. A guy like you can't figure out why a girl like me is single. And I bet your next question will be, what's wrong with you?"

He uncrossed his arms and leaned forward. He opened his mouth to speak, but she held up her hand.

"Let me help you out here. I'm single because I love my work and I'm dedicated to my patients. There's nothing wrong with me. The only reason I'm not in a relationship is because I won't waste my time and energy dating someone who-who—" she blinked hard to fight back the stinging sensation in her eyes.

He finished her sentence for her. "Someone who cheats on you with your cousin for months and breaks off your engagement when he decides he wants to marry your cousin instead of you?"

She pursed her lips. A stupid tear actually fell out of one eye.

"I'm leaving." She pushed back her chair and reached for her purse.

"Wait. I'm sorry. I can be a total jerk sometimes." He reached out quickly and grabbed her hand. He squeezed it gently. "I had an ex-girlfriend cheat on me a few years ago."

Emily hesitated. Either the shock of his hand on hers or his revelation stopped her. "Why would someone cheat on you?" He was gorgeous. But also a bit of a jerk. "Was it because—?" She stopped and bit her lip.

He smirked at her. "Were you about to ask what was wrong with me?"

She tried to pull her hand out of his, but his grip tightened. "No, I was going to say . . . well, I mean . . ."

"It was years ago. I went through a tough time. She couldn't handle that. She wasn't able to stick by when things got real. So she found a man who wasn't going through a tough time. I found out about it one day, and the rest is history." He paused and looked at her hand. "But at least I didn't get an invitation to their wedding." He looked up at her with a teasing grin.

She pulled hard and managed to get her hand out of his grip. "They probably didn't want to pay for your meal at the reception. Caterers charge based on the number of guests." She would know. She received quotes from about twenty catering companies when she thought she actually had a wedding to plan with Ethan.

"Please tell me that you requested the most expensive meal for the reception."

Emily shook her head. "Buffet."

"Is there an open bar?"

"Cash bar."

He let out a low whistle. "Is there anything redeemable about the wedding or reception?"

Ashley smirked. "It's on a boat."

Bill raised his eyebrows. "A boat?"

"The reception is a three-hour cruise around a lake. There will be no way to hide from gossiping relatives on the boat."

"Wow. This wedding sounds better and better. What lake?"

Ashley wrinkled her nose. "Lake Edwards."

He tilted his head slightly. "I don't know where that is."

She sighed. "It's actually a gorgeous location. It's a large lake tucked away in the mountains, surrounded by trees and beautiful scenery. But it's also four hours away."

Bill's jaw dropped open. He looked like he was about to say something but his gaze shifted to something behind her. He lifted his chin in a man-nod.

Emily turned, expecting to see a woman, but faced a tall man with a buzz cut. Bill stood up and gave the newcomer a handshake combined with a half hug, the way men do when they know each other well but are too manly to give actual hugs.

"Emily, this is Steve. He's the guy I told you about. He runs the restaurant now."

Emily gave him a smile. "Nice to meet you."

"It's even better to meet you." He shook her hand and then turned to Bill. "I heard you were here with a woman and had to run out here to see it with my own eyes."

Bill cleared his throat. "Yeah, well . . ."

Steve leaned in closer to Emily. "I was starting to worry about him. He's been coming here alone for the past few months. Glad to see he finally found someone who could tolerate his company."

Emily chuckled. Steve seemed pretty cool. "How do you two know each other?"

"We met at basic." Steve thumped Bill on the shoulder.

"Basic?" Emily asked.

Bill cleared his throat. "We met a long time ago before I entered medical school. We did some training together. Anyway, Steve, any specials tonight?"

There was some sort of silent conversation between them, like the conversation she tried to have with Ashley at the last restaurant. But it looked like Steve actually understood Bill's message.

"No specials tonight, just the usual. You want the ravioli or something else?" Steve asked Bill.

"The ravioli is fine for me. Emily?"

Emily looked quickly at the menu but didn't read any of the words. "The ravioli sounds great."

Emily waited for Steve to walk away before turning back

to Michael, who was now seated again. "I thought you hate eating alone?"

He rubbed his jaw. "Just because I hate eating alone doesn't mean that I can't eat alone."

"You tricked me into coming here by saying that you didn't want to eat alone. You lied."

He narrowed his eyes at her. "You said you like shrimp but you clearly lied about that."

Emily shrugged. At this point, she didn't care if he knew the reason. "I didn't want to ask you to be my date to the wedding while I had bits of spinach dip stuck in my teeth."

"So why not order something you actually like?"

She sighed. "I panicked. Anyway, it doesn't matter anymore because I'm not going to ask you to come with me. It was a bad idea."

"Why is it a bad idea?"

Emily rolled her eyes. "Because lying never leads to anything good. If I ask you to be my fake boyfriend, then I'm only going to get stuck in one lie after another until everything falls apart. Haven't you ever seen any romance movies?" He gave her a blank look and shook his head. Of course he never watched any of those movies. He probably watched action movies or superhero movies. "Anyway, fake relationships never work out."

"Plus, you can take care of the problem yourself, right?"

"Yes." She laced her fingers together. "I'm just going to go alone and keep my head held high. If it gets bad, I'll hide in some corner of the ship. And if it gets really bad, I'll jump into the water, swim to shore, and hike through the mountains for days until I make my way back to my car."

"Sounds like a reasonable plan." He tapped his cheek with his finger. "But it sounds much harder than asking me to go as your actual date instead of your fake date."

She let out an exasperated sigh. "Really? Ok, fine, Bill," she spoke each word sarcastically. "Do you want to go to a wedding next Saturday? It is four hours away, on a boat. We will spend the entire day together even though we barely know each other. We'll pretend to be happy for the married couple, who started dating while I was engaged to the groom."

He cleared his throat. "I'll check my calendar and let you know tomorrow."

Emily's mouth dropped open.

Bill looked at something behind her. "Ah, here's our food. Hope you still have an appetite."

4

EMILY

Emily steered her car to the on-ramp of the highway and slammed on her brakes to avoid hitting the car that suddenly stopped ahead of her.

"Sorry!" She glanced over at her passenger. Theresa was looking down at a large splatter of coffee spreading over her scrub pants.

Theresa grumbled something, but Emily couldn't hear her clearly.

"Did you burn yourself?"

Theresa placed her nearly empty coffee cup back into the cupholder. "It's my own fault. It was too hot, so I took off the lid. I should have been patient."

"There's another coffee shop a few blocks away from the nursing home. I'll swing by the drive-through. We have enough time." Emily bit her lip and merged into traffic on the highway.

"I'm fine. I'll just smell like coffee the rest of the day. Not that it matters."

"We can go back to the hospital for clean scrubs." Theresa didn't respond. Emily risked a look at Theresa out of the corner of her eye. She didn't know her very well since she only started working on the hospice unit about a month ago. But she knew that Theresa must spend a fortune on manicures and pedicures. She also got facials each weekend and her hair always looked perfect.

There was no way someone who was that concerned about her appearance would walk around in stained scrubs all afternoon.

"Hold on," Emily warned as she quickly shifted lanes in time to take the exit off the highway. At the next intersection, she turned back onto the highway, retracing their path back to the hospital.

Theresa made no acknowledgment of the change in plans. Emily gripped the wheel tighter. "I'll pull up to the back door. Jump out and change into clean scrubs. If we have a short lunch break today, we won't fall too far behind schedule."

They sat in silence until they pulled into the parking lot of the hospital. As promised, Emily pulled up to an employee entrance, and Theresa jumped out. Emily called the nursing home to let them know of the delay.

A few minutes later, Theresa returned to the car in clean scrubs, looking perfectly polished as always.

As Emily pulled out of the parking lot once again, Theresa sighed. "Thanks for turning back. It really didn't matter, but I appreciate it anyway."

Emily hesitated, and then spoke. "Is everything ok?"

"How do you do this job every day? The patients hate me, their families hate me, and it's depressing. All the patients are dying."

"They are going to die, but we can help them and their families during their last days. We can be a comforting presence during the hardest time of their lives. Dying is a natural part of life."

"I can't help anyone when they don't even like me."

Emily bit her lip. It was true. She couldn't ignore the way the patients and their families treated Theresa coldly while they were warm and welcoming to her.

"You just need to find a way to connect with the patients."

"That's what you said yesterday. They don't want to connect with me."

Emily tried a different tactic. "What about your previous assignment? What unit did you used to work on before transferring to hospice?"

"Cardiology."

"How did you connect with the patients there?"

"I didn't. I just took their vitals and brought them to the exam room. I'd ask them some questions and then let the doctor take over."

"Hmm. Well, why did you switch to hospice?"

"I was forced to switch. I definitely didn't request it."

Emily thought that over. "There must be a reason you decided to become a nurse in the first place."

Theresa nodded. "I thought I'd be good at it. And I thought I'd meet a rich doctor and get married."

"Oh." Emily was speechless. It shouldn't have been a surprise. There were always stories of doctors and nurses getting together. It was a classic, albeit cliché, pairing. The sexy female nurse and the gorgeous male doctor. Why couldn't it be the sexy female doctor and the gorgeous male nurse? "Did you ever think of becoming a physician instead?"

"Instead of what?" Theresa looked over at her and frowned. "Look, I'm just being honest here."

"Sorry." Emily tried to think of a way to help her. "Is there anything you like about being a nurse?"

"Not these days. Why did you become a social worker, anyway? Couldn't have been for the money."

Emily decided to ignore the condescending tone in

Theresa's question. It wasn't the first time someone questioned her career choice. Money wasn't the solution to everything. It couldn't buy happiness. "I first went to college to study biology. I wanted to be a scientist. But the classes were boring. Finally, I realized that I felt like the best version of myself when I helped other people. So I switched majors and studied social work."

"Some people can't be helped." Theresa's voice was so quiet that Emily wasn't sure she heard the words correctly.

"Hospice patients need our help more than anyone else." Emily glanced at Theresa out of the corner of her eye before continuing. "Patients see providers from hospice when they have less than six months left to live. It's up to us to help them get as much comfort and closure before they die. And we also get to help their family members. I don't think you'll ever find a job that's more meaningful than this."

Theresa said nothing, which made Emily feel frustrated and annoyed at the same time. The patients deserved better than a nurse who didn't want to be by their bedside. A familiar tingling crept up the back of Emily's neck. It was the sensation she felt whenever she suspected that a patient was hiding some sort of secret. A reason why they were so bitter.

But she needed to figure out how to get Theresa to help the hospice patients, not delve into Theresa's history. "What about hobbies? What do you do in your spare time?"

"Watch movies and do my nails. Or practice with my makeup."

Emily tried to relate to Theresa's interest but couldn't. She only used basic foundation, mascara, and lipstick. Her nails were never polished. "I'm actually going to a wedding next weekend. Do you think you could give me some tips on my makeup for it? I want to look really good."

Theresa looked her over. "Sure. I'd love to do that. What are you wearing?"

"I don't know. I'll have to buy something, I guess." Emily tried not to imagine the snide comments she'd get if she showed up in anything less than stellar. Her grandmother already accused her of not putting enough effort into her looks last Thanksgiving.

"Ok. Let's go after work today. I know of a few great places to look for dresses. And there's an amazing makeup store near one of the dress shops. This is going to be so much fun!" Theresa clapped her hands together excitedly.

"How far away is the makeup place?"

"It's about two miles from the next exit."

"Do they have nail polish there?"

"Absolutely. They carry the only brand of nail polish that I use."

"Tell me how to get there." Emily set her jaw and cut off another driver to make the exit.

"I know I said I hate this job, but I still need it." Theresa's excitement was gone, and she sounded defeated again. "We can go shopping after work. I don't want to get fired today."

Emily raised her eyebrows. "If my plan works, we won't get fired for this."

By noon, Emily was sitting at a table in the nursing home lobby, typing the last report from her morning's work on her laptop. She glanced at the clock on the wall. She would give Theresa five more minutes before dragging her out of the last patient's room.

When the five minutes ticked by, she decided to give Theresa another five minutes. After fifteen minutes passed, Emily stood up and walked over to the room where she had last seen Theresa.

Sure enough, Theresa was still sitting in the patient's

room on a folding chair next to the old woman's bed. The woman, who looked older than her eighty-five years, rested in a bed with the back elevated so that she was almost sitting. The nails on her outstretched hand looked newly painted.

Emily cleared her throat quietly, not really wanting to interrupt their time together. But there were more patients on their schedule.

Theresa glanced up at her and grinned like a child who was caught red-handed. "Sorry, we got carried away chatting." She looked back at the patient. "Liza, I'll be back in two days to check on you."

Liza gave Theresa a large grin and held up her hand. "Hope you bring some more nail polish."

Theresa winked. "I'll bring more colors for you to choose from."

As Emily and Theresa walked out of the nursing home, Theresa stopped and gave Emily a huge bear hug.

"What was that for?" Emily asked, trying not to sound too surprised.

"Well, just . . . I don't know. I mean, thank you." Theresa blushed slightly as she spoke.

"You did it all yourself. You just needed a little push to connect with her."

"Yeah, well, I didn't think it would be possible even with a push."

Emily opened her car door and climbed inside. She started the car, switched gears into drive, and then looked over at Theresa. "We barely have enough time to pick up lunch before our next patient. We'll have to eat in the car."

A phone call notification from an unknown number appeared on her car's screen, which usually meant a telemarketer or a patient's family needed her. She answered it and waited for the recorded message that was sure to follow.

Bill's deep voice filled her car. "Hello, Emily?"

5

EMILY

Emily slammed the breaks, which was not necessary since she hadn't pressed the gas pedal and the car was barely moving. She jerked forward, then shifted the car into park. "Ouch, um, hi Bill." She glanced at Theresa and moaned. "Theresa, I'm so sorry."

Theresa stared at the contents of her water bottle, which were now all over her scrubs and Emily's front seat.

"At least it's water this time."

"I'll bring you back to the hospital to get dry scrubs. Maybe you should grab a second pair in case something else happens like this today."

"We don't have time for that." Theresa looked on the floor, then leaned over and peered into the back of the car. "Do you have a towel or something?"

Emily reached out to the glove compartment and pulled out a handful of small napkins. "That's the best I can do."

Theresa dabbed her shirt with the napkin and gave up almost immediately. "I'm going to run back inside and try to dry off in the bathroom. I'll be back as soon as I can."

Emily watched her exit the car. It was impossible to tell if

Theresa was clumsy or if she was an exceptionally bad driver today. Either way, she should ban drinking or eating in her car. Or at least require all riders to bring their own changes of clothes.

She started humming a song while she waited for Theresa to return.

She had to admit, it was nice having Theresa along with her today. The previous hospice nurse frequently went on rounds with her, and she missed having the company. Maybe she shouldn't have judged Theresa so quickly. But to be fair, Theresa had been pretty annoying. She always complained and asked Emily to do her work for her.

Maybe today was the start of a new beginning for Theresa. Maybe she'd start to like working with hospice patients as much as Emily did.

A male voice floating over her car's speakers jerked her out of her thoughts. "Emily?"

Bill! "Oh no, I completely forgot that you were on the phone." She cringed. "Did you hear all that?"

"Yes."

"And?"

"And what?"

She exhaled. "Nothing."

"Are you alone in the car now?"

She wrinkled her eyebrows together. Why would that matter? "Yes."

"You could have just asked me to call back later. I feel bad for whoever was in the car with you. What did you do? Soak her with water?"

"No. She spilled it on herself. I had nothing to do with it." Well, almost nothing. She only overreacted to the sound of his voice and slammed on the brakes like a beginning driver who was scared of the car's shadow.

"I need more information about the wedding next weekend."

"Fine. I'll call you later with the details."

"Can you just give them to me now?"

"What do you want to know?"

"What time is the ceremony?"

"I don't know. Maybe around 3 p.m. The cruise will start about an hour afterward." She squeezed her eyes shut and pinched the bridge of her nose. "The cruise will last for about three hours."

"And what's the name of the location?"

"Lake Edwards." This was worse than the childhood game of twenty questions. "Look, I have to get going. I'll call you later with more information."

"Is your friend back in the car already?"

She frowned. "No."

"If you want me to go, I need a few more details so I can clear my schedule for the weekend. Do we need to book a hotel room? What time do you want to leave?"

Emily pursed her lips, refusing to think of how many dates he'd have lined up for a typical weekend.

"Does this mean you'll actually come with me?" *Or are you just trying to get my hopes up?* Emily hated that she was actually holding her breath, waiting for his answer.

"That depends. If I make a few phone calls, I'll be free to go with you. But before I agree, I have a few conditions."

Conditions? Only she would have the bad luck to catch a playboy who was also high-maintenance. "What are they?"

"First, I'm driving. We take my car. I choose the music."

"No."

"No? That's only the first condition," he said.

"I'm driving. You can pick the music, and you can choose whose car we take, but I'm going to drive."

"Non-negotiable, Emily. I drive or I don't go."

"Is this a guy thing? You don't think a woman can drive as well as you? Because I have to tell you, I've never been pulled over by police. I've never had a ticket." There had been one car accident, but she wasn't at fault—no need to mention that.

"Neither have I."

She tried another tactic. "I'm not about to get in a car with a guy I barely know and let him drive. For all I know, you'll murder me in the middle of a forest."

"I won't. And if you think I would, then why would you ask me to the wedding?" An edge of frustration crept into his voice.

She bit her lip. If the wedding was four hours away, she'd definitely be carsick by the time they got there Saturday morning. She would not survive the wedding and reception if she was sick before it started.

"Fine. You drive. But we have to leave Friday night."

"That's a detail that would have been good for me to know at the beginning of the conversation." His voice was now sarcastic. He might not be worth taking to the wedding after all.

"Well, now you know. We'll leave Friday after work, stay at a hotel near the wedding location, and you get to drive."

There was silence at the other end.

"Does all that work for you, or are you going to change your mind?"

He cleared his throat. "That works." His voice sounded strained. He cleared his throat again. "Let's get together for coffee tomorrow morning, and we'll figure out all the other details for the weekend. I'll text you the address of the coffee shop."

"Fine." She paused. "And, um . . . thank you."

"You're welcome."

She jumped slightly as Theresa opened the car door. Her

scrubs looked mostly dry. Theresa started talking animatedly before she even climbed in the car. "They had electric air driers in the staff bathroom, so I managed to get mostly dry. But anyway, I'm so excited about dress shopping after work today! I just remembered this gorgeous dress that I saw last week, and I think the color would be perfect on you. It's backless, so you can't wear a bra, which isn't a problem. Are your boobs real or fake? Because if they are fake, then you might not need extra support, but if they are real, then we can stop by this amazing lingerie shop. So, real or fake boobs?"

Emily stared at Theresa, speechless and eyes wide. She shook her head.

The voice floated over the car speaker again, deep and husky, like he was straining to get the words out. "I'll give you the rest of my conditions tomorrow morning, Emily."

6

BILL

"Your next patient called. He's running late. Should be here in about twenty minutes."

Bill nodded at the aid, and she left, closing his office door behind her.

He leaned back in his chair. Twenty minutes. Twenty to get the sound of Emily's voice out of his mind. To erase the desire to see her in a backless dress. To stop imagining the silky feel of her skin as he ran his fingers over her back, holding her close to him during a slow song on the rocking boat.

This weekend was going to be a mistake. Denying that fact would be pointless. He'd only seen Emily a handful of times since his best friend, Michael, started dating her cousin, Ashley. Each time, she had the strangest effect on him. He had trouble coming up with the right things to say, he had trouble keeping his focus, he had trouble functioning like a normal person. A person like Emily wasn't someone he could casually date.

He tried to ignore her appeal. They couldn't be together, and he'd be the type of guy he'd sworn never to be if he led her on, only to break up with her when she learned the truth about his life.

He nearly broke his promise to himself to stay away from Emily a few weeks ago when she showed up at the same hospital fundraiser that he'd attended. Instead of asking her to dance to each song with him, he spent the night flirting with other women. It didn't work. He couldn't get Emily out of his thoughts.

And now she asked him to spend a weekend with her. An entire weekend. Two days with her. It was a mistake, and a better man would ignore the temptation to get closer and run away before he hurt her.

His phone buzzed, jolting him out of his daydream and nearly sending him flying backward in his chair.

He grabbed his phone. If Emily thought she could convince him to let her drive, she'd quickly learn that was a fight she'd never win.

His shoulders tensed as he read the name of the caller. It wasn't Emily.

"Julie, this better be important." He cringed as he heard the tone of his voice.

"Don't you dare make it sound like my calls aren't important." Julie's words were rushed, the way she spoke when stressed.

"You've called me about six times this morning. If it were so important, you would have left a voicemail."

"You have responsibilities here. You can't make me handle everything on my own. You promised me that you'd be here to help."

"I have been there to help. Every single weekend for the past year."

"For the past ten months. That's not a year."

He looked up at the ceiling and tried to find an ounce of

patience. He softened his voice. "Fine. Ten months. You win. Happy? I can't go next weekend."

"What am I supposed to tell them? They ask about you every day." Her words tumbled out faster than before.

"Tell them the truth. That I have other things to do this weekend, but I'll be back next weekend, like usual."

"You know that won't work."

"Then I'm out of ideas. I don't know what else to say."

"Say that you'll face your responsibilities and move here."

His jaw dropped. He opened his mouth to speak, but nothing worked.

"Hello? Are you still there?" She sounded even more annoyed.

He barely managed to speak. "You know I would move there if I could."

"You can. You just don't want to."

"The only hospital within commuting distance is a small, regional facility. They don't need any cardiologists there."

"You are a doctor. You can practice general medicine. You're smart enough to figure something out." The words would have been a compliment if they came from anyone except Julie.

He instinctively picked up the contract laying on his desk. All he needed to do was sign on the line, and he'd be the newest addition to the Clareville County Hospital. One signature and he could throw away years of performing complicated, lifesaving open-heart surgeries for days filled with diagnosing rashes and sore throats.

"Bill," Julie's voice was quieter, gentler. Bill tensed. "I know it isn't what you want, but we need you here. It's too much for me to handle alone."

He rubbed his temple with his free hand. Julie knew how to get what she wanted. "Jules, I—"

"Just don't say no yet. Come here this weekend. I'll find

someone to watch them Saturday night so you can hang out with some of your old friends. You'll still get the break that you need."

"I have to be somewhere this weekend. A wedding."

"Where is the wedding?"

"Lake Edwards."

"That's just thirty minutes from me. From Clareville." She sounded hurt.

"No, not Lake Eddard. Lake Edward-*s*."

"I don't even know where that is."

"About three hours' drive from here. I looked it up on a map. It's in the opposite direction from you."

Julie took a heavy breath. He could picture how she looked. If she was home, she was probably pacing in the backyard, away from curious ears. A bird singing in the background confirmed his suspicion.

"I'll change my work schedule and arrange a four-day weekend next month."

"That doesn't solve anything." She sounded mad again, hurt. "One or two extra days every few months is not a solution. I need you here. You have a responsibility here."

"Julie." He tensed, ready for another fight.

"Fine. You take this weekend for yourself." She paused for several seconds. "You haven't even asked me how they are doing."

He sighed and made a fist. He silently pounded it on the desk. "How are they doing this morning?"

"Not well. Dad refused to eat his breakfast and his blood sugar dipped too low. Mom got really anxious. She keeps asking when you'll be here. Plus, Luanne showed up forty-five minutes late, so I was late to work." Luanne was the less-than-dependable home health aide who was hired to come during the week.

he spoke.

"Yes. That's why I really need you here, all the time, and
not just weekends."

"I'm doing the best I can." He looked at the contract in
front of him. He wasn't doing the best he could. Yet.

"Whatever. I have to go. Have fun at the wedding this
weekend." She hung up on him.

He dropped his phone on his desk. He was about to sign
away his years of cardiology work. His freedom. Why didn't
his sister understand that? One lousy weekend was all he
asked for. One weekend to pretend that he wasn't suffocating
under the pain of watching his parents decline with dementia. One weekend to act like he had a normal life, with the
freedom to date the woman he'd been thinking about for
weeks, and nothing better to do than take an impromptu trip
to a lake tucked away in the mountains.

He grabbed his pen and scribbled his signature on the line
at the bottom of the contract, signing away his chance to
have a future with Emily.

7

EMILY

Emily was on time. He wasn't. Which was fine with her. She smiled in gratitude as the guy behind the counter handed her a cup of coffee. If Bill decided to back out, then she could still ask that guy to go to the wedding with her. He wasn't nearly as tall as Bill and was more scrawny than muscular. He also looked several years younger than her. But that didn't really matter. All that mattered was that she had a man next to her at the wedding.

He could be her barista boyfriend for the weekend. Had a nice, poetic sound to it. Barista Boy. Barista Boy on a boat. Or was he a baristo?

The guy behind the counter looked at her again with a concerned expression. "Are you still waiting for your order?"

Her cheeks grew hot, and she shook her head. "No, sorry, thanks. Hey, are you a barista or a baristo?"

He narrowed his eyes. "Excuse me?"

"I was just wondering what the proper term was for your job. Are you a barista or a baristo?"

He looked at the line forming behind the register and then back at her, his face expressionless. "Barista. The term is

Italian and refers to anyone of any gender who serves the coffee." He turned around and walked away without saying anything else.

Emily watched him go. Well, at least she'd know how to introduce him to the other wedding guests if it came to that. He seemed a little annoyed by the question, though. She doubted he'd be willing to go with her, seeing how they just had their longest conversation, and it went poorly.

She reluctantly turned around and started scanning the room for an empty table. The early morning crowd meant that most of the tables were full, but there were still a few options.

The table closest to the door was open. So was another table in the middle of the room. And there were several empty seats at a long bar placed against the window. Those seats were the best for people-watching, which was one of Emily's favorite hobbies. She promptly walked to one of the empty chairs, sat in one, and put her purse in the chair next to hers to save it for Bill.

It was the perfect spot for their meeting. She could people-watch, and he wouldn't be able to constantly scan the room for a more attractive woman to flirt with.

Her coffee had just cooled enough to sip without burning her tongue when Bill walked up to her. He had his phone up to his ear but removed it briefly to address her.

"Sorry I'm late. I have to finish this phone call. It will be about another minute or two. Get me a cup of coffee? Cream, no sugar. Then we can talk." He dropped a five-dollar bill on the table in front of her.

She frowned. She wasn't here to serve him. He could get his own cup of coffee if he wanted it. She opened her mouth to protest, but he was already walking away, absorbed in the phone call.

She grabbed the money and walked up to the counter.

There were three people ahead of her in line, and none of them seemed to know what they wanted to order. By the time it was finally her turn, she had trouble returning the smile of the woman at the register.

"Back again so soon?"

"Yeah. Can I get a cup of coffee for my friend?"

"Sure. Do you want cream and sugar?"

"Cream, no sugar." She handed over the cash. "Wait! I meant sugar, no cream."

The woman paused, hand hovering over the register screen. "Which is it?"

Emily took a deep breath and ignored the twinge of her conscience. He definitely said he wanted cream in his coffee. "Extra sugar. No cream."

"One coffee with lots of sugar, coming right up." She handed Emily the ticket number, and Emily stepped to the section of the counter where the drink would be placed. She waited barely a minute before the same male barista called her name, holding out the hot drink. He gave her a curious look.

"Thanks, this one is for my friend."

He shrugged and walked away.

A large glass container of sugar sat on the counter. Just for good measure, she dumped a stream of sugar into his coffee, stirred it carefully, and then walked back to their chairs.

Except he wasn't there. Her coffee was gone too. There were now other people sitting in their seats.

She clenched her jaw. He left? And now she was stuck with a cup of coffee with enough sugar to cause instant cavities.

She walked up to the woman sitting in her seat. "Excuse me, I was sitting there and just got up to get coffee for my friend."

The woman turned around and faced her. "He's back there." She nodded towards the back of the café.

"Excuse me?"

"He asked me to switch tables with him. He's in the back corner, with your coffee."

"Thanks." Emily looked in the direction the woman was pointing and saw Bill sitting at a small round table, seated with his back against the wall with a clear view of the café.

He gave her a small wave and smirked.

She set her shoulders and walked over to him. He was probably the worst type of playboy she'd seen. He couldn't even handle sitting together for one cup of coffee without sitting in a spot where he could check out any attractive women in the room.

Well, things would be different at the wedding.

She sat down opposite him and put his coffee next to her. "My choice of seats isn't good enough for you?"

"I never said that."

"You made another person switch seats with you." She crossed her arms.

"I don't like people-watching." He nudged her cup of coffee. "I brought your coffee over for you."

She watched him carefully. "Why did you change seats?"

"That topic again?" He shifted his weight in his chair slightly. "This table is better. If we are going to work out our plans for the weekend, then this table offers more privacy. Less chance of anyone overhearing us."

Emily narrowed her eyes. Why would she care if anyone heard their conversation? The café was noisy enough that it would be hard for others to overhear. Even if they did, where was the harm in that? It wasn't as though they were doing anything unusual or illegal.

"Fine. Let's get this started." She moved his cup of coffee

over to his side of the table. "There's no change. I left it as a tip."

"That's fine."

"Ok." Ugh. Since when was talking to a guy so hard? She licked her lips. "So, about the wedding . . ."

"Did you bring a copy of the invitation, like I asked?"

She nodded and reached into her purse. She placed the invitation on the table and slid it over to him. She pretended to take a sip of coffee while watching him from under her eyelashes.

His brow furrowed as he read the invitation. "You said it was at Lake Edwards."

She nodded.

He turned the invitation around and slid it across the table so it was in front of her again. "Read that part." He kept his finger on a section about halfway down the page.

She looked. Her heart skipped a beat. Lake Eddard. Oops. "Does it matter? It's just a different lake."

"That lake is a five-hour drive from here."

She pursed her lips. "Good thing we are already planning on getting hotel rooms Friday night. I can drive if the distance is too far for you."

He set his jaw and looked at her with fierce eyes. "I drive. My car, my music. We already agreed to that."

"Fine. But I hold on to the key at any stops we make," she countered.

"Why?"

"In case you turn out to be a creep. I can get away while you are in the bathroom."

"If I were a creep, I wouldn't let you out of my sight at any stops. I would just go to the bathroom on the side of the road."

"You are gross."

"But I'm not a creep."

She stared at him, refusing to even blink.

He exhaled. "Fine. I drive, and you get the key each time we stop."

"Deal." She reached out her hand to shake his.

He leaned back and crossed his arms across his chest. "That's not my only term. We have more work to do."

She matched his movement and leaned back, crossing her arms. "What do you want?"

"I want to book the hotel rooms."

She could allow that. "I'll pay for my room, and you can book them. But we have to stay at the hotel listed on the invitation. My family is expecting me to be there."

"What's your budget for the room?"

"Why do you need to know?"

"I don't want to get the most expensive room if you can't afford it."

"Then don't book the most expensive room. And, I can afford to pay for the hotel." He wasn't the only adult sitting at the table who had a job.

"Fine. I'll book the rooms. You pay for yours, and I'll pay for mine."

Emily started to nod in agreement and then stopped. "That won't work. We'll need to share a room."

He raised his eyebrows and his face showed much more than just a hint of a smile. "Just because I'm coming with you doesn't mean that we are . . ." He let the sentence hang and wiggled his eyebrows at her suggestively.

"Don't get dirty with me! I mean—" she looked away for a second to clear her head "—if I'm taking you there as a date, no one will believe that we are actually together if we have separate rooms. So, we are sharing a room."

He wiped the smile from his face. "Fine. One room, one bed."

"Two beds."

He gave a subtle nod. "Next condition. I'll be by your side, as your boyfriend, from the time we get there until the time we leave, with the exception of Saturday morning."

She narrowed her gaze. "What does that mean?"

"You don't ask any questions about it. I'll be back at the hotel by noon, ready to be your boyfriend. Since the wedding doesn't start until three, it shouldn't cause any problems."

She frowned and considered his words. "Fine. I have some terms of my own."

"I haven't finished telling you about mine."

"Then take a break from your list and listen to mine. While we are there, you act like my boyfriend. You do not flirt with any other woman. You do not hook up with any other woman. You do not get to dance with any other woman."

He nodded. "I didn't expect you to be the jealous, controlling type."

She broke eye contact and looked down. "I'm not. I just can't stand the thought of another round of humiliation if my 'boyfriend'," she raised her fingers in air quotes, "cheats on me at the wedding of my cheating ex-fiancé."

He was silent for a minute. "Agreed. Ready for my next condition?" He waited for her to nod. "While we are there, you act like my girlfriend. You do not flirt with any other man. You do not hook up with any other man. You do not get to dance with any other man." His voice echoed her tone as he repeated the same words she said.

She took a sip of her coffee while she considered how to respond. "Are you making fun of me?"

He shook his head and mimicked her actions, taking a sip of his own coffee. Emily watched carefully to see how he'd react to his drink. He paused, licked his lips, and took another tentative sip.

"Ok, I agree to those terms," she said.

"Any other rules you want to make before we return to my list?"

She raised her chin to him. "I don't know how to phrase this, exactly." She raised her hand to her mouth. "We'll need to probably, um, *kiss* during the reception. Act like we are in love."

He nodded. "Sure. What else?"

"That's all you have to say about that?" She'd been worrying about broaching that topic during their entire conversation, and he reacted as if she just suggested that they sit at the same table. "Fine. I'm done. Your turn."

He checked his watch. "I'll make this quick. First, I want to see you in that backless dress at the reception. Second, I've been dying to know if your breasts are real or fake ever since you had that conversation with your friend yesterday. Third, do not put sugar in my coffee again." He leaned forward so his face was inches from hers.

She leaned forward to shorten the gap between them. "First, I will wear what I want to wear." She bought the backless dress last night because Theresa had been right. It looked amazing on her, and she wanted, more than ever, to look amazing for the reception. But that wasn't any of his business.

"Second," she continued, "I'm only going to answer that question because you are doing me a favor and I don't want you to ask over and over again. They are definitely real. Third, don't order me to get your coffee if you want it a certain way." She pushed back her chair and grabbed her purse. "I have to get to work. I'll see you Friday evening. Pick me up at five and don't be late."

With that, she walked away without bothering to look back at him.

8

BILL

Bill pulled up to the building and double-checked the address. He expected a nicer building. It wasn't bad, exactly, but it wasn't as well-maintained as his apartment building. Without even getting out of the car, he could tell that the apartment building lobby wouldn't have marble inlays on the floor or a concierge. The best this building had to offer in terms of amenities would be an elevator. He'd be shocked if there was even a security system.

He exited his car and walked three steps towards the entrance before something in the corner of his eye caught his attention. He turned slowly and looked at the car parked to his right. Someone was hefting a large suitcase into the trunk.

Her back was to him, but he recognized the natural red highlights in her dark hair. He turned his body so he faced the owner of the vehicle and crossed his arms. When the owner finally managed to push the suitcase into the trunk, he cleared his throat loudly.

The vehicle owner jumped slightly and turned in his direction. A satisfied grin slowly transformed into the look of someone who got caught doing something wrong. The transformation intrigued Bill more than he expected.

He watched silently as she shifted her weight from foot to foot, wondering how she'd react next. Finally, she looked away briefly and ran her hand through her hair. When she looked back at him, she had a large smile plastered on her face.

"You came a few minutes early. I'm almost done loading my car. It will be easier if I drive. Or, if you really have to, drive separately." She rolled her eyes. "We can each drive our own cars."

He frowned. She had a huge stubborn streak, which would probably only worsen if he let her know how much this attracted him. Besides, he would not start his last weekend of freedom with the same solitary drive down the path that led to Clareville and his parents' house. Not when he had an option to spend the next few hours with a woman like her.

He walked over to her car, brushing up against her as he approached her trunk. She gasped, but he ignored her. Instead, he pulled her suitcase out with one hand and reached for a large tote bag that had already been placed in the trunk.

"If there's anything else that's supposed to come with us this weekend, grab it now."

"Wait, Bill—"

"You agreed. I drive, in my car."

She jogged up to him and stepped in his path. He stopped and stared at her again. "We agreed that you can drive your car. Nothing changed there. We never agreed that I would drive up with you."

An edge of amusement threatened his resolve to look serious. He tried not to let the corners of his mouth rise. She had no idea that her relentless determination made her even more attractive. Maybe he should let her drive separately. They were only fake dating, and he needed to remember that.

But she gave him another glare and any thought about driving separately disappeared. He would win this game.

He shrugged his shoulders in mock defeat and turned back to her car. He tossed the tote bag and suitcase in her trunk and then closed the door.

"I'm not interested in a kidnapping. You can travel in whichever vehicle you want. I'll be in my car. Just let me know what I'm supposed to tell all your relatives when they ask why we came separately."

That did the trick. He saw the conflict start in her eyes. She chewed her lip silently while he waited to see what she would decide. She opened her mouth slightly, but no words came out. She clearly didn't know if it would be worse to give in and ride in his car or stand her ground and take her own. He knew what he wanted.

He took a step backward towards his car. "See you at the hotel, cupcake."

He turned around so she wouldn't see his face. He almost made it to his car before she caught up with him.

"Wait!" She placed her hand on his bicep and he turned around obligingly. "What did you just call me?" She did not look amused, standing with her hands on her hips.

"Cupcake." He shrugged. "I also considered calling you sugar lips or sugar pie. Or sugar." He reached out and moved a stray lock of her hair that had fallen in her face. He let his fingers linger on her face a second longer than necessary. "Don't you ever use nicknames in a relationship? I thought a sugary nickname would be perfect for you since you put sugar in my coffee."

She frowned and held up a finger. "First, I hate those nicknames. Do not call me by any of those names. Second, I-

I-I . . ." She wrinkled her nose and let out a loud gasp. "Fine. I don't have a second point. Let's just leave and get through this weekend."

She reached into her purse and pulled out the wedding invitation, holding it out to him. "The address is on the card."

Shoot. She still planned on taking her own car. He stepped forward as if to take the invitation but wrapped his arms around her, enveloping her in a large bear hug. "Aww, don't be mad, honeybun. Or should I call you cuddle cake? I'm glad we're having this conversation now, privately, instead of at the wedding reception." He silently swore at her ex-fiancé. Bill could tell she didn't want to trust him, and he'd bet good money that it was because her ex was a cheater who didn't know how to treat someone like Emily the way she deserved to be treated. If he couldn't get her to trust him long enough to get in the car, he'd never earn her trust.

"Don't call me honeybun or anything else." Her voice came out slightly muffled against his chest.

"We could get to know each other much better if we actually rode in the same car. But since we're going separately, I guess we can have some get-to-know-you conversations at the wedding. I hope nobody asks any prying questions about our relationship. As you can see, I'm really bad at improvisation." He gave her one last squeeze before releasing her from the hug. He reached for his car door again. "I'll see you up there."

She stood, motionless, as he opened his car door and climbed in. She really was more stubborn than he had anticipated. He turned on the car, put it in reverse, and started backing out of the parking space. There was no way he was actually going to leave, but did she know that too? He took one last glance at her. She stood in the same spot, looking miserable.

He stopped the car and rolled down the window,

watching her closely. Playing games wasn't winning her over. He needed a new plan. Honesty. His voice became serious. "Look, I have a great driving record. I never drive under the influence. I promise that I'll go the speed limit, or slower, if that's what you want."

She hesitated and glanced one last time at her car. "We really need to convince everyone that we are a real couple this weekend. If they realize that I just asked a random guy to come with me, then I'll be a huge laughingstock. I want to make it through this weekend." She chewed her lip.

"Then stick your bags in my car. I'd let you drive my car but . . ." He shouldn't have even started that sentence. There was no possible way he'd get in a car with anyone other than himself as the driver. "I promise I'll behave, and we can learn everything about each other on the drive there. We will be a real couple this weekend."

She gave a small nod. "Fine."

She barely finished speaking the word before Bill turned off the car and jumped out. He walked back to her car and transferred everything to his trunk, taking the bags out of her hands each time she tried to help. For a two-night trip, she packed a lot. He really wanted to ask why she needed so many bags but knew better. If having a sister taught him anything, it was never to question someone's packing techniques.

Finally, they were both settled in the front seat of his car, ready to leave. He turned to her before starting the car again. "Ready to leave, schmoopie?"

She faced him. "Ready, teddy bear." A small smirk crossed her face.

9

EMILY

Emily watched the clock. She'd made it through forty-five minutes in the car before feeling the familiar signs of motion sickness. She reached forward and adjusted the temperature in the car again. The cool air blew directly on her face but offered little relief.

She shivered and rubbed her arms. A roadside sign indicated that there was a gas station up ahead. If she could get out of the car for a few minutes, then she might not feel so sick. Plus, she made the mistake of putting her bag with the ginger ale and crackers in the trunk. She blamed Bill for that mistake. The way he looked and talked to her made her confused. She could barely think straight with him around, much less remember how to organize her luggage in his car. "Let's stop at the next exit."

Bill glanced at her briefly before looking back to the road ahead. "We haven't even been on the road for an hour."

"It's healthy to stop and stretch on long car rides."

"I'm pretty sure they don't mean to stop every half hour."

"We left forty-five minutes ago, and I guess that I just assumed a *doctor* would be interested in healthy habits."

Despite the nausea, she smiled. There was something about this man that kept her on her toes. She liked how his jaw clenched when she egged him on. It was like he couldn't tell whether to laugh or yell. Either way, he looked undeniably good. Another wave of nausea washed over her. "I left a few things in the trunk by mistake, and I'm starting to feel carsick. If we stop soon, the ginger ale and crackers might help before things get too bad."

She watched his face, but his expression remained clear of any emotion. He moved his head slightly as he checked the mirrors, and he carefully pulled the car off to the side of the highway.

"What are you doing? I can wait until we get to the exit."

He put on the hazard lights and turned to her. "I'm not going to make you wait. We can still stop at that next exit. Which bag has your snacks?"

She described the bag and watched as he got out of the car and went to the trunk. Moments later, he reappeared with the bag.

"Need anything else?"

She shook her head.

He got back into the car and carefully pulled back onto the highway. She took a tentative sip of the ginger ale and tried to stare at the horizon.

After a few minutes of silence, Bill spoke. "You didn't tell me that you get motion sickness."

"You didn't ask."

"Isn't that the type of thing a boyfriend would know before going on a long trip?"

She shrugged. "I guess so. Now you know."

"Did you take any medicine before we left?"

She rolled her eyes. Boyfriend or not, there was no excuse for him to treat her like a child. "Yes. I always take it but it doesn't work. That's why I wanted to drive."

He sighed. "I'm sorry. I didn't mean to make you suffer."

She took another sip of ginger ale. "It's not your fault." Except it was his fault. He was the one who demanded to drive.

"What medicine did you take?"

Emily glanced at him briefly before pulling the bottle out of her purse. "It only helps to take off the edge of the nausea."

He looked at the box briefly. "Have you ever tried any prescription medicine for motion sickness?"

She licked her lips and adjusted the air vent again. "No." The thought never even crossed her mind.

"This is good." He nodded his head while she narrowed her eyes at him. "We are getting to know each other. This is something that I should know as your boyfriend. You get car sick and you like ginger ale."

She groaned. "If that's all that you know about me by the time of the wedding, we are in trouble." She took one more sip of the ginger ale before looking for the cupholder in his car. There was already a travel mug in the cupholder closest to her seat and a metal water bottle in the other one. He glanced at her.

"You can move my water bottle. But be careful with the travel mug and don't close the lid to it. There's a fish in there."

"A what?"

"It's a little beta fish."

Emily studied the horizon again and considered her words carefully. "Is this a special pet of yours? What's his name?"

"Boo Boo. Well, actually, I guess he's Boo Boo the Second."

"Oh." The nausea was coming back stronger now. If they stopped at the next gas station, she could call Ashley from the bathroom and beg her to come pick her up. Or hire a car to drive her back home. This was weird, right? What kind of grown man would take his pet fish, named Boo Boo the Second, on a weekend trip? "He must be a very special pet."

Bill clenched his jaw the same way he did in the parking lot earlier.

Emily reached for a cracker with her free hand. "I don't have any pets, but I have a lot of clients who consider their pets part of the family. Like a child." She didn't mention that the pets were usually cats or dogs. Not fish. "Do you, um, have a special bond with this fish?"

A shot of laughter came out of Bill's mouth. "You think I'm crazy, don't you?"

"No."

"I'm not crazy. I promise. This fish is a gift for someone."

She let out a deep breath. "Do you have friends near Lake Eddard?"

He stopped laughing and checked the rearview mirror before responding. "I know some people up there."

She nodded. It really was none of her business who he knew there, and she didn't want to pry. "That's nice."

"Do you still want to stop at this exit?"

She shook her head. "The ginger ale helped. We can keep driving. Unless you're willing to stop and let me drive the rest of the way?" Emily crossed her fingers while she waited for his response.

He pursed his lips and shook his head slightly. "How do you plan on getting through the boat ride tomorrow?"

"I'll do the best I can."

"What does that mean?"

"If it gets bad, I'll hide in a corner of the ship."

"And what should I do after you disappear at the reception?"

"Hide with me?" The words came out as more of a question than a statement. Emily couldn't picture Bill hiding from anything. She also couldn't picture the humiliation if he started flirting with the bridesmaids while she hid in the corner with a stash of ginger ale.

"Won't everyone think that we are . . . you know?"

She sighed. "Of course they will. But how would it look if I showed up to my ex-fiancé's wedding and was sick for the entire thing?" Emily cringed. "Honestly, I just want this weekend to be over. I don't even know what I'd do if you hadn't agreed to come with me. I can't thank you enough." Emily swallowed hard as she said those words. She hadn't exactly made the trip easy on him so far.

He took his hand off the steering wheel and placed it gently on her knee. It felt almost platonic. Almost. "If we are being honest, I could use some time off. I'm looking forward to getting away for the weekend," he said.

She stared at his hand on her knee. She was about to place her hand on top of his when he withdrew it and placed it back on the steering wheel.

She shook her head to clear her thoughts. "So we finally agree on something."

"We do?"

She paused and replayed his previous words in her mind. They didn't actually agree on anything. He didn't actually say that he was looking forward to being with her for the weekend. "Never mind."

He placed his hand back on her knee and gave it a gentle squeeze. "I think—"

"We still need to figure out our fake relationship. And learn about each other so we don't make any mistakes at the wedding."

He removed his hand from her leg and cleared his throat. "Right. Do you have any allergies?"

"No. You?" That wasn't the first question she would have thought to ask, but she was willing to answer it anyway.

"Penicillin and some seafood. Are you on any medication?"

"That's a personal question."

He shrugged. "Isn't that something a boyfriend would know?"

"Maybe. But it's not a topic that's likely to come up while we are all hanging around the buffet at the reception."

"Fine. Any current health conditions?"

"I'm healthy. And this is not a doctor's appointment, even if you are a doctor. So shift topics, please." She thought for a second. "Where did you grow up?"

"Not too far away from here."

"Do you have any siblings?"

He shrugged. "A sister. You?"

"No. I just have my cousin, Ashley, who is practically a sister."

"Why isn't she coming to the wedding?"

"Wrong side of the family. She's not close to this side of my family."

A silence filled the air. Emily chewed her bottom lip. It had been too long since she was in the getting-to-know-you phase of a relationship. How was this supposed to work? She could ask about hobbies, but she didn't want to hear about his dating life. Maybe she could ask about where he went to medical school since he was a doctor. But this was a date, not a job interview. Or was it really a date?

If it was a date, it was a fake date. A pretend date. A date with no future. So it didn't really matter if she impressed him. As long as he was willing to play the role that he agreed to play for the wedding tomorrow, then it didn't matter if she bored him to tears. Besides, how could she possibly say anything that would impress a guy like him anyway, a playboy who could date any woman he wanted?

She sent up a silent prayer that he would remember his

promise not to flirt with anyone at the wedding. She wasn't naïve enough to think that some of the single women—and possibly some of the non-single women—at the wedding, wouldn't try to hit on him. If Ethan was any indicator of the moral beliefs of his family, cheating was not only appropriate but encouraged. So it would be no surprise if Ethan's female relatives all jumped at the chance to steal Bill away.

It would be pure humiliation and torture if her "boyfriend" was caught cheating on her at the wedding of her cheating ex-fiancé.

She should have found a less handsome man to take with her. That wouldn't have been hard. Practically any man was less attractive than Bill.

Why couldn't Ashley have known of a less attractive guy without playboy tendencies to set her up with for the weekend? Better yet, what was so wrong with her that she even needed to pretend to have a boyfriend?

She and Ethan broke up about four months ago, after all. That should have been plenty of time to get over the heartbreak and start dating again. It was obviously more than enough time for Ethan.

But Ethan was a creep who didn't know the meaning of love. She would actually feel sorry for her cousin, the bride-to-be, if her cousin wasn't equally horrible. Veronica was just a year older than she was but picked on her relentlessly throughout her childhood. It was even worse during her awkward teenage years. Somehow, Veronica managed to avoid the years of pimples and thick eyeglasses. Veronica even looked good in braces, unlike Emily, who couldn't master speaking without a lisp during the entire two years of wearing them.

But stealing her fiancé was worse than Emily ever expected.

Her stomach started rolling again as the car continued to

speed along the highway. She glanced over at Bill, who silently mouthed the words to the song playing quietly on the radio.

She shifted in her seat and Bill glanced at her. "Do you mind if we just listen to music? I'm really feeling sick." She took a last sip of the ginger ale and then leaned her head back, eyes closed. "You can pick out whatever music you want."

He said nothing but turned up the music as a new song started to play. She recognized the slow beat and cringed. It was their song. The song that she and Ethan first danced to, the song that they played every time they cooked together. It was the song that Ethan had paid the band to play the evening he took her to the outdoor concert and proposed. She always pictured getting engaged in a private, intimate moment, like at the top of a secluded mountain after a long hike or during a picnic at a serene park. His proposal at the concert wasn't what she imagined, and she felt completely awkward as the entire concert audience stared at her, and the lead singer cheered them on, but she couldn't deny that some women would think it was romantic.

Ethan ruined her love for that song forever.

She opened her eyes. "Can you skip this song?"

"You don't like it? It's one of my favorites."

"I hate it."

He shrugged. "You said I could choose the music." He stole a glance at her, with a playful half-grin. "Do you always back out of your promises?"

He sounded like he was trying to tease her, but she wasn't in the mood. Her head was starting to hurt, the nausea was returning, and she still had hours to get through before they reached the hotel. She covered her ears with her hands. "It's fine. Do what you want. I'll just—"

He interrupted her by putting his hand back on her knee. "You know, I think I hate this song now too. It's pretty bad."

"You aren't serious. You just said you love it."

"How can anyone love this song? The beat is too fast and the lyrics are too repetitive." He started drumming his hand on her knee in rhythm with the song. "See? My hand is already getting tired from moving so much."

The corners of her lips threatened to turn up, despite the nausea. "You are a bad liar. You love this song. How else would you know all the words?"

He started singing loudly, still keeping beat to the song by tapping her knee. She covered her ears again, laughing, which only made him sing more animatedly.

When the song was finally about to end, a text appeared on the car's display screen. He was singing so animatedly that he didn't notice the text.

But she did.

Will I see you tonight?

BILL

He pulled up to an empty space in the parking lot in front of the hotel. The sun had set long ago, and the large hotel was lit up. He'd never been there before, but the manicured landscaping and pristine exterior offered a hint of the luxury within the resort.

A soft snore came from the passenger seat. Emily had fallen asleep after their last stop, about an hour ago.

He suspected that her motion sickness was worse than she admitted. She barely kept up with the conversation while she was awake, and he lost count of how many times they stopped along the way.

He got out of the car and closed his door gently. He took a few steps towards the hotel entrance, enough to see a glimpse of the expansive lobby filled with comfortable sofas and chairs. He hesitated.

The resort looked safe, but safety could be an illusion.

He could walk inside and check-in, leaving her in the car to sleep. But night had fallen hours ago, and the resort was surrounded by woods, miles from the main road. He strained his neck to look inside the hotel again. He couldn't see the check-in counter from this position, which meant that he wouldn't be able to keep an eye on the car while checking in. If he couldn't make visual contact with the car, and her asleep in the car, then he couldn't leave her alone.

He surveyed the lot. There were no closer spots to park. The hotel had a circular driveway up to the entrance, where cars could park while unloading baggage and checking in. However, there were already several cars there. If he were to pull up there, not only would multiple people walk by the car with her asleep, but there was also a high potential that he'd get blocked in by another car.

That wouldn't work. He always needed a clear escape route for his vehicle.

That left him with only one choice.

He walked to the passenger side and opened the door, prepared to catch her or anything else that might fall out once her door opened. He held his breath, watching her carefully. She stirred briefly but remained asleep.

He leaned over her and unbuckled her seatbelt, ignoring the heat radiating off her body. He held his breath again, gingerly putting one arm behind her back, the other under her legs, and lifted her out of the car.

She stirred again and mumbled something that he couldn't understand.

He paused, but she remained asleep.

He pushed the car door closed with his hip and walked towards the entrance. The baggage could wait. Once he had safely deposited her in the hotel room, where she could sleep without risk, he'd return for the bags.

She stirred again in his arms, nestling her head against his neck. He took a deep inhale. Big mistake. She smelled intoxicating. He gripped her closer, which was another big mistake.

Every inch of him ached to protect her. She looked so

vulnerable. She looked completely opposite from the woman who had faced him at her apartment hours earlier. He couldn't tell which side of her intrigued him more.

None of that mattered, though. He had a job to do this weekend, which was to be her boyfriend. After that, their relationship would end, and he'd move back to his hometown, back to help his parents and his sister, Julie.

He reached the entrance to the hotel and walked into the lobby. There was a double-sided fireplace in the middle of the large lobby with a roaring fire to fight off the chill in the spring air. Sofas and armchairs were placed throughout of room, and about half of them were occupied.

After a few glances around the room, he found a group of chairs against a wall that was within eyesight of the check-in counter.

He made it halfway to the chair when a loud shriek caught his attention. He tightened his grip on Emily and turned around, eyes narrowed.

A tall, older woman with bright red lipstick and a tight dress motioned to him frantically from across the room. She rushed over to them, making enough noise to wake the dead.

Emily stirred against his chest and opened her eyes.

"Wha—Bill? Where are we?" Her voice was thick with sleep.

"Just about to check into the hotel. You know that woman?" He adjusted his stance so she could see the woman who was quickly closing the distance between them.

Emily stiffened in his arms. "Oh no, that's my mom, Cheryl. Quick, let me down!" She patted his shoulder.

He held on to her tighter. "Nope. I'm not letting go. I'm your boyfriend, remember?" A better guy would have probably released her, but he couldn't. Not yet.

"No, just put me down—" She patted him harder. He

winked back, hoping to see the spark in her eyes. He needed to make sure that her nap eased the carsickness.

"Just watch and see. You wanted a boyfriend, well, you got a boyfriend." He glanced up to see that Emily's mother had nearly reached them. Just for good measure, he gave Emily a quick kiss on the cheek. "Cheryl! So glad to meet you. I'd shake your hand, but my hands are a bit full at the moment." He flashed a smile at the woman now standing in front of them, a look of surprise on her face.

Cheryl blinked. "And you are . . .?"

"Bill, of course." He flashed her the smile that had melted many hearts over the years.

"Bill, this is my mother, Cheryl. Mom, this is Bill, my um . . . my boyfriend." Emily wiggled again in Bill's arms, trying to get out of his grasp.

Bill laughed. "Sorry, Cheryl. You've caught us in the middle of a small disagreement. My driving made Emily a little carsick, so I insisted on taking care of her and carrying her inside. She thinks she can walk, but . . ." He shrugged for good measure and gave Emily another quick kiss on the check. "You know Emily. She can be awfully stubborn."

He could see Cheryl practically swoon. "Emily," she admonished, "you should let him help you. He does look very strong, after all."

Emily stopped wiggling and sighed. "Fine. If you insist on carrying me, Bill, put me down in that chair, and we can be done with all this." She pointed to a nearby grouping of chairs in the middle of the room.

"Fine." He walked in the opposite direction to the grouping of seats that he had originally noticed. Two of the chairs were backed up against a wall, while a small sofa was opposite the chairs. Cheryl followed and sat in one of the chairs while he placed Emily on the sofa.

"Hmph. Thanks." Emily muttered weakly with a frown.

He leaned in over her and placed his forehead against hers. "Anytime, girlfriend."

She finally cracked a small smile. "Thanks," she said again, with warmth behind the words.

Fully aware of her mother's watchful presence, he gave her a kiss on the forehead before standing up and heading to the check-in counter.

He kept a watchful eye on Emily and her mother while checking in at the counter. Emily still looked pale, but he couldn't tell if that was from the lighting or from the car ride. But he didn't like how tense she appeared while talking with her mother. Within moments, another woman joined them. She looked around the same age as Cheryl. Possibly an aunt or older cousin. He narrowed his eyes at Emily, who looked like she wanted to disappear into her chair.

He forced his gaze from Emily and tried to focus on checking into the room quickly. A sign next to the counter caught his attention from the corner of his eye. He motioned to the sign and spoke quickly to the woman at the counter. Finally, she handed him two hotel keys and a printed schedule for the morning.

He walked back to the small group, unnoticed by any of the women until he sat down next to Emily. She gave him a quick glance before reaching for his hand. He took her hand in his and gave it a light squeeze.

"Bill, meet my aunt Peggy. She's the mother-of-the-bride." Emily did a remarkable job of keeping a smile on her face as she spoke. A week ago, he wouldn't have known that the smile was fake.

"Peggy, so nice to meet you. Your daughter picked a beautiful hotel, and I'm sure the wedding will be just as nice." He flashed his best smile at Peggy while wrapping his arm around Emily.

Peggy made a small *tsk* sound and shook her head gently.

"It's so nice to see that Emily found a friend to come with her this weekend so she's not all alone. You know—" she lowered her voice to a false whisper "—we all thought Emily would marry Ethan. Of course, we were all shocked when the truth came out about Ethan and Veronica. I guess you can't stop true love, can you?" She leaned back with a smug smile on her face.

"Sorry, I think you misunderstood. I'm definitely not just a friend," he said. To emphasize the point, he pulled Emily closer and laid his other hand on her knee. Then, for good measure, he kissed her on the cheek. She blushed but didn't pull away, which was exactly the reaction he wanted. Instead, she leaned against him and placed her hand on top of his.

"Ah, well, isn't that sweet?" Peggy's voice still reeked with pity.

They hadn't even been at the hotel for more than ten minutes, and Bill could already see why Emily had been so relentless in her search to find someone to take to the wedding. At least Emily had chosen the right man. She wanted a boyfriend, and he would fill that role for as long as possible.

Peggy placed a hand dramatically over her heart. "Anyway, Veronica still feels so bad for you and is so happy that you decided to come. She asked me to invite you to spend the entire morning with the bridal party. They are going to meet for breakfast, fix their hair and makeup, get ready together, and have the pictures taken by the photographer. She said that you could come and help them with anything they need. Get them coffee, help zip-up dresses, run any last-minute errands, that sort of thing. Isn't that nice? I never thought Veronica would want to include you, but you know Veronica. Always quick to forgive and forget." Peggy alternated her glance between Cheryl and Emily.

Cheryl's face contorted into an odd smile. Similar to the

smile Emily gave when she felt uncomfortable. "I'm sure Emily has other plans."

"Forgive and forget what, exactly?" Bill's voice came out louder than he anticipated as he looked between the women.

"Let's just say that Emily and Veronica never saw eye-to-eye on Ethan—especially after she found out that Ethan loved Veronica. Emily said some, well, less-than-ladylike things when she found out. We don't blame her, though. But I do wonder what kind of person would try to stand in the way of other peoples' happiness." Peggy's words made Bill want to pick Emily up and take her back to the car. "Veronica is expecting you at 8 a.m. Stop by the lobby café on your way to her room and bring them the drinks on this list." Peggy pulled out a small sheet of paper as she spoke and held it out to Emily.

Bill glanced at Emily. She looked worse than she had during the drive up. She blinked several times. "Aunt Peggy, thanks for the invitation, but I—"

"Peggy, please send Veronica our regrets that Emily can't come in the morning. She has plans," Bill said. He knew he should let Emily handle this but couldn't stop himself.

Peggy put the paper on the small table next to Emily. "Veronica specifically invited you. She said she needed someone to run errands or hold things for her. You can't say no to a bride on her wedding day."

Bill tried not to scowl at the absurdity of the thought of Emily running around, doing her cousin's bidding. "She is not available." He held Peggy's gaze.

Emily shifted slightly. "Thanks again for the offer, but—"

"What is so important that she can't even help her own cousin?" Peggy didn't attempt to hide the irritation in her voice as she refused to look at Emily and addressed Bill.

"She has an appointment at the spa," he said. "Facial, manicure, pedicure, and hot stone massage."

"She can't afford that. This is a nice hotel," Peggy argued.

"She can definitely afford it. She's an incredible social worker. But that's beside the point. It's my treat for her. She deserves a morning of indulgence." He held Emily close as he spoke.

A slight gasp came from her mother. Good. That was exactly the reaction he was hoping for. He hadn't planned on showing off his surprise for Emily, but her aunt's insistence didn't bring out the best in him.

He waited for Peggy to show a sign of reaction. She sat there, arms crossed against her chest. At least she didn't look like she pitied Emily anymore.

"Well, if she can't be around to help in the morning, tell me your room number. I'm sure Veronica and Ethan will want to stop by to welcome her. Plus, Veronica will drop off supplies for making the centerpieces for the reception. She ran out of time since planning a wedding is *so* stressful. I'm sure that Emily won't object to putting together the arrangements for the tables." The smug look returned to Peggy's face.

Bill counted to five before he responded. This woman had nerve. After a five-hour drive, Emily was not going to stay up late to assemble decorations for a cheating ex-fiancé's wedding. He plastered on his best smile again. "Sure. It's room 1002. Tenth floor."

He watched with amusement as Peggy's forehead wrinkled. "There isn't a tenth floor. We all have rooms on the top floor, and that's the eighth floor."

Bill shrugged and held up the key so they could see the room number. "The top two floors require a special elevator, around the corner. Restricted access. Only works with a room key." Emily gave him a questioning look. "Executive floor. They have the best suites." Not to mention a secure elevator.

Emily mouthed the word *thanks* and yawned. "We should probably head to our room and get unpacked. I'll see you both tomorrow." Emily slipped out of his arms and stood up. He followed immediately.

"Cheryl, Peggy, nice to meet both of you." He nodded at each. Cheryl stood up and gave Emily a hug while Peggy sat, frowning.

Cheryl turned to Bill and embraced him in a hug. She whispered in his ear, quiet enough that no one else could hear. "I don't know who you really are, but thanks for coming. Take care of Emily this weekend. She acts strong, but I worry about her. We were all a bit surprised at how things turned out."

She released him from the hug, and he gave her a curt nod. From the look on Cheryl's face, he realized that this weekend was going to be challenging for her, as well.

Bill and Emily made it to the elevator before Peggy caught up with them. "Wait a minute! How will Ethan and Veronica get the decoration supplies to you? You need to put those centerpieces together tonight since you aren't going to help tomorrow."

Bill grabbed Emily's hand tightly before facing Peggy. Emily opened her mouth to speak, but he didn't care. "Emily can't help with the decorations. She's here as a guest, not help. Besides . . ." he pulled Emily in close to his side possessively. "She's mine for the weekend, and I don't plan on sharing her."

The elevator dinged behind them and the doors opened. He took a last glance at Peggy, just in time to see a tall, athletic man walk over.

Ethan DeGraus.

Bill locked eyes with the man. His stomach churned. He vaguely felt a hand on his chest and looked down. Emily stood in front of him, trying to push him back to the elevator. Her mouth was moving and she was saying something to him, but he couldn't hear her.

All he could think about was that snake. He took one last glance at Ethan and turned, letting Emily lead him into the elevator.

11

EMILY

As soon as the elevator door closed, Emily hit the button for the tenth floor and closed her eyes, exhaling loudly. She tried to let go of Bill's hand, but he had a death grip on it.

"Well, at least that's done. We saw Peggy and Ethan. My mom seems enamored with you already, so that's good. And I can't thank you enough for giving me an excuse to avoid Veronica tomorrow morning. I guess I can just spend the morning in the room. There must be a movie or something I can watch on TV. I also brought a bottle of clear nail polish in case my pantyhose gets a run, so I can paint my nails and say it's a manicure and pedicure." She was rambling by this point but couldn't stop herself. Being alone with Bill in the car was one thing. Holding his hand in the elevator, moments after he played the role of her personal hero, was another.

She took another deep breath in before continuing. "How much did the room cost? I didn't realize that they had a floor with a private elevator, but I can't imagine it was cheap. I know I said I could afford a room at this hotel, but this is more luxurious than I expected." she paused, biting her lip.

She always said too much when she was nervous. "Never mind. I'm sure I can cover the cost of the room. It definitely impressed my aunt and mom."

He finally turned to her as if he had forgotten that he was also capable of speaking. "I didn't get the room to impress anyone. The hotel said that there are only three suites on the tenth floor, and only guests in those suites can access the rooms. I like my privacy."

"Oh. Ok." The elevator dinged and the doors opened to the tenth floor. She stepped out first and starting walking down the hallway. "What's our room number?"

She stopped walking when she realized he wasn't behind her. She turned around and saw him by the elevator, arms crossed against his broad chest. She paused.

"1002. This way." He jerked his head in the opposite direction. She backtracked and walked by him, not stopping until she reached the correct door. "Key?" She held out her hand.

He ignored her and reached past, inserting the hotel key card into the slot and opening the door. He immediately turned on the lights and walked through the large suite, opening and closing each door before checking the locks on all the windows.

She watched him silently. When he finished the inspection, he turned around and faced her. She stood still in the middle of the room, suddenly aware of his overwhelming presence in the suite. It was larger than a standard hotel room, with an arrangement of sofas and chairs in one room and a door leading to a bedroom. But somehow, it felt too small for both of them.

She shivered involuntarily and rubbed her arms. "It's a really nice room. Thanks for booking it."

"Like I said, I wanted a private room."

"Right." She paused and bit her lip. "If you give me a room key and your car keys, I'll go get the suitcases from your car."

He exhaled loudly, a mix between a laugh and a sigh of frustration. He shook his head. "I'll get them. You stay here." He took two steps towards the door and then paused, shaking his head. He turned back around and faced her. He was no longer smiling but looked intensely serious. "You never told me you were engaged to Ethan DeGraus."

She crossed her arms and lifted her chin. "I told you that. I didn't hide anything. Why does it matter?"

"You told me that his name was Ethan. You never said his last name was DeGraus."

"I guess I didn't think of mentioning it. But you saw the invitation."

He shook his head. "I didn't."

"Yes, you did." She walked to her purse and pulled out the invitation, which was the same paper she showed him a few days ago. "Remember? I thought the wedding was at Lake Edwards. I showed you the invitation, and you pointed out that the wedding was at Lake Eddard. See?" She stepped close enough to him to hold the invitation up in front of his face. "His name is right here, clear as day."

He leaned forward and looked at the invitation. His face was getting redder by the second, and a vein had popped out on his forehead. She held her breath, not sure what to say. He was obviously mad about something, but she hadn't lied.

He finally looked back at her, looking like an entirely different man than the one who had flawlessly impressed her mother moments ago in the lobby. Everything about his body was hard and tense. His eyes were steely, with no sign of humor around the corners. Even though his gaze landed on her, she felt like his mind was a million miles away.

He looked like he'd seen a ghost.

"Bill?" She spoke the word quietly, not sure if she should

bring his attention back to her and the room, or let him stay lost in his thoughts for a few more moments.

He blinked hard and shook before grabbing the invitation from her and crumbling it into a ball with his hand.

"You ok?" A thin line of sweat ran across his brow. She didn't remember seeing that when they'd been in the lobby, or in the elevator.

He gave her a curt nod and turned toward the door of their suite. "I'm getting the luggage. Stay here."

12

EMILY

"Stay here?" Emily repeated Bill's words to the closed door. Did he really think he needed to throw out commands like that?

If it weren't for the change in his personality and appearance after seeing Ethan's name on the invitation, she would have been seriously annoyed with the causal manner in which he threw out a command before letting the door close behind him.

But why had he acted so strange? Ethan was a creep, but it wasn't like Ethan ever hurt Bill the way he'd hurt her. Unless Ethan stole a girlfriend from Bill? But even if that happened, why would Bill look like he'd seen a ghost after reading his name on the invitation?

And even more importantly, why did she feel guilt creeping over herself? She'd shown him the invitation a few times. Doesn't anyone attending a wedding look at the name of the bride and groom? She had no idea that he knew Ethan. Ethan never mentioned anyone named Bill while they were together.

The nauseous feeling from the car ride returned to her stomach.

Emily made her way through the suite until she reached the large bathroom. A porcelain white bathtub rested next to an enormous shower, large enough to fit more than two people. A flush of heat rose to Emily's cheeks as she turned away from the shower.

She shouldn't be thinking of Bill in that way. He practically ran out of the room minutes ago, and he'd made it very clear that he came to this wedding as a favor. Or did he? Anyway, it didn't matter if he came as a favor or not. She wasn't going to get involved with anyone. No matter how attractive he was.

The shower did look inviting, with crisp white towels arranged neatly on the shelf. Two white robes hung from a hook on the opposite wall. Emily opened the glass shower door and turned on the water, letting the water reach the perfect temperature.

By the time Emily stepped out of the shower and wrapped herself in the bathrobe that was so fluffy it must have been made by angels, rustling noise floated in from the bedroom. She opened the door to see Bill arranging their suitcases in the large walk-in closet.

She crossed her arms. "Everything ok?"

He finished unloading the luggage cart and pushed it into the hallway. He let the door to their suite close behind him, leaving her alone in the room with him again.

"I brought you some food." He pointed to the luggage. Sure enough, there was a takeout bag of food from the hotel restaurant. "I figured you wouldn't want to go to the restaurant and risk seeing any more relatives. Looks like I guessed correctly." His eyes roamed over her bathrobe.

She tightened the robe and crossed her arms. "I don't want to pry, but you looked upset before you left."

"We should eat this before it gets cold."

She studied his face, but his eyes masked all emotion. Emily bit her tongue and walked over to the table, tentatively opening the first of several bags, still watching him.

"I promise, there's no shrimp."

She tried to hide the smile that crept onto her face and looked deeper into the bag. It smelled good and her stomach gave a loud growl.

She turned to face him. He did promise to come to the wedding, and she needed to make sure that there wasn't going to be a scene between him and Ethan at the wedding. There couldn't be any drama tomorrow. As much as she wanted to leave him alone with his thoughts, she couldn't. "How do you know Ethan?"

"Doesn't matter." He walked over to her and removed the bag of food from her hand. "I'm hungry. Let's eat. Do you want to get dressed first?" He eyed her bathrobe again.

She shrugged, refusing to feel weak. "I want to know how you know Ethan first."

He turned his back to her as he looked through the suite's kitchen. After opening the third set of cabinets, he pulled out two plates and then shuffled through the drawers until he found some silverware. He turned back around to her.

She waited for a response, but he didn't say anything.

"Were you and Ethan friends?"

He put the dishes on the small dining table.

"Did he steal an ex-girlfriend from you?"

Again, no response.

She bit her lip. "Did he date your mom? Is he your stepfather or something?"

Finally, she got a reaction. Whether he meant to or not, a small snort escaped his lips. He turned back to the counter.

"Oh, I know!" She snapped her fingers. "You're actually an

undercover cop and weaseled your way into coming to this wedding so you can arrest Ethan and send him to jail for the next fifty years."

He finally turned around and looked directly at her.

She inhaled deeply. "I'm not giving up until I know the truth."

A knot formed in her stomach as his look intensified. He looked ready to pounce.

"This is crazy." He focused directly on her eyes as he spoke, without a hint of a smile on his face.

She tried her best not to squirm and crossed her arms as she took a step closer. "You are the crazy one if you think you can ignore me. I asked a question, and I want an answer. How do you know Ethan?"

He crossed his arms and took a step closer to her, copying her moves. "I never said I could ignore you."

She fought the urge to swallow hard, blink, or show any other sign of weakness. "How do you know Ethan?"

He took another step closer. "It doesn't matter."

"It does." She matched his step but covered less ground this time. She needed to keep some distance.

"We met, some things happened, and we parted ways." He took another step closer.

"That's the story of every relationship that ever happened." She raised her chin in order to not break eye contact as she took another step towards him.

"Is that our story?" He put his hand under her chin, cupping it slightly.

"You are trying to distract me." She brushed his hand away from her face. He rested it on her shoulder instead.

"Isn't that what a good boyfriend does?" He placed his other hand on her other shoulder.

She tried not to break eye contact. He needed to learn

that he couldn't just use his charm on her like he probably did on all his girlfriends. Other women might throw themselves at him, but not her.

"A good boyfriend respects the woman he's with. A good boyfriend doesn't act the part in front of someone's relatives and then refuse to talk behind closed doors, when there is obviously some history between you and him." He winced as she spoke, but she didn't feel any pleasure.

"A good girlfriend doesn't force her boyfriend to talk."

She let out a huff of air. "I need to know that there won't be trouble tomorrow. I can't handle anything embarrassing at the wedding."

The corner of his mouth edged up a fraction of an inch. "I promise you that I will be your perfect boyfriend. All weekend."

Her face grew hot as she realized that she was staring at his mouth. She immediately lifted her chin again so she could focus on his eyes, and he shifted closer at the same moment. Her heart pounded in her chest.

He took advantage of her silence.

"Tomorrow morning, we'll make an appearance at breakfast before I need to leave. I'll be back in time for the wedding."

"Fine." She looked at his mouth again. Why did he have to be so attractive? Maybe she should just do it. Kiss him. Right here and now. But he already ran away once. He might not even be interested in her like that.

She pried her eyes away from his lips and looked at his eyes again. "There's just one problem."

"What's that?" His mouth tensed.

"You know the right things to *say* in front of my relatives, but there was more to our agreement than just that."

"Hmm?"

She tilted her head slightly and shifted her weight. "You agreed that we'd kiss a few times at the reception. You know, to make sure everyone was convinced that we are really dating."

"I haven't forgotten. What's the problem?"

She tried her best to look stern. "I don't want to be embarrassed in front of everyone if you are a bad kisser." She held her breath.

"Are you asking me to kiss you now?" He raised his hand to cup her cheek, drawing her face closer to his.

Instead of answering, she closed her eyes. His lips were a fraction of an inch away from hers, almost touching. All it would take was one small movement and his lips would be pressed against hers.

He probably knew how to kiss. A man who looked like he did must know how to kiss. But she hadn't kissed anyone since Ethan. And in her entire life, she'd only kissed one other man besides Ethan. Would she even know how to kiss someone who wasn't her ex?

Emily cringed and pulled back.

How could she think about Ethan at a time like this? That lying, cheating piece of scum couldn't even be upfront with her and end their relationship. Instead, she spent weeks planning their wedding while he dated countless other women, including her own cousin.

And now Bill. Did she really have to repeat her mistakes in order to learn the lesson? She pretended not to see all the texts he received on the drive here, or the time he took to call a woman at one of their rest stops along the way. He and Ethan were nearly the same: playboys who couldn't commit. Ethan just hid his actions better.

She turned away from Bill and sat primly at the table. "Never mind. Bad idea. We can deal with the kissing issue tomorrow. I'm hungry." She checked to make sure that her bathrobe was still firmly secured around her before opening the first container of food. It looked like some type of pasta dish with vegetables, and it smelled delicious. She looked at Bill. "Ready to eat?"

13

BILL

Bill sat down opposite Emily. She carefully piled some food on her plate before passing the container to him. He placed some food on his own plate and began eating.

What in the world just happened between them? She acted like she wanted a kiss. In fact, she practically demanded that he kiss her. And then she turned into an ice queen. No woman had ever complained about his kissing ability in the past. And she didn't even give him a chance. Instead, she built a solid rock wall around her.

He should never have come with her for the weekend. Or at least, he should have checked the invitation more carefully. But how could he have known that this wedding was for Ethan DeGraus?

Or, E.D., as they used to call him. *Erectile Dysfunction.* They were all so immature back then, barely out of high school. He didn't even know who started calling Ethan by that nickname. Not him. But after the first week of basic training for the military, no one bothered to call him Ethan anymore. Just E.D.

He speared a chunk of broccoli and chewed carefully.

Emily still hadn't said anything, even though she kept glancing up at him.

He ate until he was finished, then leaned back in the chair. He studied Emily's face openly. She, however, now refused to look at him. He never saw someone so interested in their food.

Did she feel embarrassed? He couldn't read her emotions. Her face remained blank. She could be mad or just hungry. But the walls she built around herself were a mile high.

She really should put on some clothes. Her bathrobe was tied tight—too tight. Even though she pulled away from their kiss, he wanted more. He hadn't actually gone on a date for months, not since his life grew complicated and he needed to be available to help care for his parents. His playboy days were gone. Or maybe he just realized, somewhere along the way, that there was more to life than going on date after date and never looking for a bigger commitment.

He could see himself being committed to Emily. That is, if she stopped comparing him to Ethan. A man like Ethan should have never been allowed to date Emily. She deserved someone better.

Like him. Or at least, the version of him that existed before his parents couldn't take care of themselves anymore. Back when he wasn't planning on moving far enough away to end any chance of a relationship with Emily. He didn't want a long-distance relationship. And, based on how she was cheated on by Ethan, he doubted she'd want to risk a long-term relationship either.

At least he could look forward to kissing her at the wedding tomorrow. Unless she changed her mind again.

Finally, she took the last bite on her plate and started to stand.

"Wait. Please," he said, trying not to sound too desperate. This could be his last chance to get through some of her walls before they were surrounded by guests at the wedding tomorrow.

"What?" She gave him a look that sent shivers down his spine.

"I have a rule. Never go to bed angry."

"I'm not angry."

"You've barely spoken to me since we started eating."

"I was hungry."

He watched her closely as she lowered her gaze. "My rule just changed. Never sleep in the same hotel room with the person who doesn't want to talk with me."

"Then get another room."

"All the rooms on this floor are booked."

"Go on another floor."

"The other floors aren't as secure." He tensed his jaw. He didn't mean to let that slip. Maybe she didn't notice.

"Why are you so concerned about security? You could probably beat up anyone in a fight."

He could practically feel her eyes roaming over his chest and arms as she spoke. That meant he could distract her and move away from the topic of security. He flexed his muscles just for good measure. She rolled her eyes and looked away.

"I bet Ethan wouldn't mind letting you sleep in his room tonight. It's probably not too late to head to the bar and hit on a few women." She didn't look at him while she spoke.

"Why would I do something like that when I'm here with my girlfriend?"

"I'm not your girlfriend."

"You are for the weekend. That was the agreement. Remember? No lying. We are officially dating."

She let out a loud exhale. "Guys like you are why girls like me give up on dating."

"That's not fair. You hardly know me. I've been the perfect boyfriend since we started dating a few hours ago."

She narrowed her eyes at him. "Are you going to tell me how you know Ethan?"

"You don't need to worry about that. It's no big deal. Ancient history."

"Ancient history? No big deal? You sound just like Ethan. 'Don't worry about it, Emily. It was no big deal. Just a momentary lapse in judgement. Ancient history. The details of what happened aren't important.' "

"That's different."

" 'I'm different now, Emily. It will never happen again. I learned my lesson. I'm better now. You are the one for me, I promise. I can't even look at another woman when you are around.' "

He felt like she'd punched him in the gut. What he really wanted to do was punch Ethan in the gut if he actually said those things to her. He softened his voice. "Don't blame me for what he did to you."

"And now you sound like Veronica. Did you know that she came to my house the same night I discovered everything and dumped him? She tried to make it sound like I tried to keep her and Ethan apart."

"That's messed up."

He watched her blink a few times in rapid succession. Her eyes looked red and watery, and she wouldn't make eye contact with him. His chest tightened. He didn't know how to handle crying. His sister rarely cried, and he never saw his mom or dad cry. Patients cried sometimes, but that was different. He usually just grabbed a nurse to help him when a patient cried or offered to refer the patient to social work. He glanced around. Should he give her tissues? Or hug her? Or pretend she wasn't crying?

She reached up to wipe one of her eyes.

He looked at the table for something, anything. A few after-dinner mints were stashed in the bag. He'd picked up a handful before leaving the restaurant with their food. He shoved his hand inside the bag and curled his fingers around the first hard object he felt.

He pulled his hand out of the bag and tossed the mint to Emily. "Here."

She looked up just as it bounced off her forehead and landed on the table in front of her. She hadn't even tried to catch it.

"What's wrong with you?" She practically spat out the words.

"I-I thought you'd catch it. You know, mints sometimes help when you feel upset." He made up the last part.

"Oh. Um . . . thanks." She grabbed the mint, unwrapped it, and shoved it in her mouth.

He watched her suck on the mint candy for a few seconds before turning away. He picked up their dirty dishes, rinsed them off in the sink in their suite, and placed them in the small dishwasher. He turned back to her.

She still sat at the table, head in her hands. Luckily, she wasn't watching him. But he couldn't tell if she was crying.

He turned back to the dishwasher and pretended to adjust the settings on it, which was stupid because there were only two plates, two forks, and two knives in the dishwasher. He wasn't going to run the dishwasher when it was practically empty.

He glanced over his shoulder again, and she returned his look.

Swallowing, he turned around, facing her again. "Did the mint help?"

She shrugged. "I'm fine."

She looked miserable.

Maybe the kind, empathetic route would get her to stop crying. "Look, people like Ethan just don't know a good thing when they see it. Trust me, the man is not someone you should have married." He watched her cautiously.

Nope. Wrong move. She lowered her head to her hands again and sniffled quietly.

"That's the problem. He knew how to be a great boyfriend. He treated me well, he helped me when I needed him, and he . . . he . . ." She stopped talking.

Warning bells went off in his head. This was worse than running into Ethan in the lobby. If he didn't do something, she'd cry all night.

A small voice of caution rose from his conscience. He couldn't let himself get caught up in her tears. He promised Julie. His family needed him. Emily had no place in his future.

Men like Ethan broke promises. Men like Bill made sacrifices.

But he still had one last weekend before reality caught up to him. He ignored his inner voice and walked over to Emily, placing a hand on her shoulder. He lowered his voice to the tone that made more than one patient look at him with eyes full of trust. "You deserve better than Ethan. Believe me, you would have seen his true colors sooner or later. At least you found out his true nature before you married him."

She let out a quiet sob as she stood up and turned to him, pressing her face against his chest and allowing him to hug her. He flexed his abs and squeezed her gently, but enough so that she'd have to notice how many muscles he had under his shirt. An ounce of distraction worked wonders with helping his patients get through tough moments. He didn't flex his muscles to distract his patients, but Emily wasn't a patient.

Finally, she pulled back slightly and looked up at him. "Thanks." She took a deep breath in. "That's what my friends said to me. I'm glad you came with me. At least I'll have one friend at the reception."

He cleared his throat and raised her chin with his finger. "Boyfriend. I'm your boyfriend."

"Right." She sounded too casual. "I can't tell you how much that means to me. I mean, not every guy would agree to this. Especially since I haven't really made this trip very easy for you so far."

He pulled her close to his chest again, wrapped his arms around her, and took a deep inhale. Her hair smelled good. Like lavender or jasmine or something flowery that women used in their shampoo.

She shifted her head slightly against his chest. He waited while she took a shaky inhale and exhale. "Seeing Ethan get married is really bringing out the worst in me. Ugh, he could have at least waited a few more months before marrying her. Or eloped, so I wouldn't have to show up at the wedding." She stopped talking, her face pressed against his chest.

He started patting her back and swallowed. He couldn't tell if she was crying. "We can always leave in the morning. You don't have to go if you don't want to."

She let out a quiet groan, possibly a sob? He could feel his blood pressure rising by the minute. No one, especially Ethan, should make Emily cry.

He tried again. "If you knew everything about Ethan, you'd have run away from him long ago." Or would she? Maybe she did know what Ethan had done and didn't care. He furrowed his brow as he considered that. She moved her head against his chest, and he wrapped his arms around her tighter.

She wriggled under his embrace and pulled back, looking into his eyes. "What did he do?"

He frowned. He should have known better than to bring it up again. She had distracted him and made him drop his guard. That never happened. "It's more like what he didn't do. I promise I'll tell you someday, but not now."

"Is it something so bad that we should tell Veronica? Is he a criminal or a murderer or something?"

He looked at the ceiling briefly before facing her again. "No. It's not that bad. But you deserve better."

Her eyes started to well up again. He shifted his weight uncomfortably. He said the wrong thing. Again. If he kept this up, she'd cry all night. He didn't know whether to keep holding her, or run out of the room before he said the wrong thing and made her more upset.

Someone needed to write a book on what men were supposed to say when a woman was upset. He knew everything to know about the human heart. He studied cardiology for years, and held countless hearts in his hand during complicated surgeries. But a woman's heart? Complete mystery.

She didn't seem to notice his mounting alarm. Emily pulled back from him again, wiping her eyes. He let her go this time. As long as she didn't completely break down in tears, he'd let her do anything she wanted.

She finally stopped rubbing her eyes and looked at him, wrapping her arms around her own body. "Look, it's been a long day. Maybe we should go to—oh no, I messed up your shirt!" She reached her hand out to his chest.

He looked down to see wet marks on his shirt where her face had been moments earlier. "That's ok. I brought other shirts with me."

She pulled her hand back and her eyes widened. "I have an idea. Since you gave up your weekend to come to this wedding, I can return the favor."

He liked the sound of that.

"I can set you up on a date with one of my friends."

His stomach dropped.

She continued, oblivious to his reaction. "There's a nurse I know, Theresa. She just started working with me a few weeks ago. She's gorgeous. Blonde hair, really tall, she's really pretty. I'm sure she'd love to go on a date with you. She's probably just your type."

What did that mean? Just his type? And why would Emily want to set him up on a date?

His chest constricted, and he lost his breath as the realization sunk in.

She wanted to put him in the friend zone.

Warning bells rang in his ears. He racked his mind for something to say to get him out of the friend zone.

He groaned. He couldn't think of anything better to do. She'd be angry, but he could deal with anger.

If she was angry at him, he could still win her over. If she thought of him as a friend . . . he shuddered at the mere idea.

Before she could say anything, he crossed his arms and looked at her critically. "As your *boyfriend* for the weekend, I'm tired and want to go to bed. It's past midnight." He steeled himself and slowly ran his eyes up and down her body. "I hope your pajamas aren't as frumpy as that bathrobe."

A hint of fire appeared behind her eyes. "That's rude."

"Sometimes the truth hurts." He shrugged and ran his eyes up and down her curves again, slowly and obviously. "If you want everyone to think I'm your boyfriend tomorrow, you should dress and act like you belong with me. Wear something to breakfast that shows off your assets. Something sexy. Something tight. Low cut." He settled his eyes on her chest.

She reached out and slapped him. He didn't even see it coming.

Warmth spread through his cheek. It stung mildly but didn't hurt. He rubbed his jaw as he opened and closed his mouth carefully, as if the slap might have done actual damage to his bones.

Emily stared at him, mouth open and looking shocked.

A grin threatened to break out across his face. He bent over slightly as though in pain.

"You know you deserved that." She stood up tall.

He rubbed his cheek again, for good measure. He focused on narrowing his eyes so he wouldn't crack and smile like a fool. She did not look like she was about to cry, and she definitely didn't look like she thought of him as a friend.

He took a step forward, fully aware of how much he towered over her. He dropped his voice to a whisper. "If you knew what I was thinking right now, there's no way you would stop at just one slap." He winked and turned around before she could respond.

EMILY

Emily stared at the door to the bedroom. Did he really just say that? And did she really just slap him?

She had never slapped anyone in her life. Not even Ethan. He also never said or did anything like Bill just did. He cheated on her behind her back. Bill, however . . . Bill was a player. He probably always looked at women like that. Like they were something he wanted to devour. Like he had nothing else he'd rather do than . . .

She shook her head. She needed to clear her mind. She needed to get the image of Bill out of her brain.

He was a friend and nothing else. Maybe not even a friend. After this weekend ended, she'd never have to see him again. He could be free to continue dating woman after woman, and she'd be a distant memory.

And maybe one day, in a few months or years, she'd be ready to date someone. She'd find a nice, boring guy. A man who might not get a second glance from women at the bar but still knew how to hold a conversation. A man who was average.

Not Bill. Definitely not Bill. He looked too good, his

muscles too big, his chest too hard. Women drooled over men like him based on looks alone. She'd have to fight off the competition constantly if she actually dated Bill. He was gorgeous, rich, intelligent.

And he was a jerk. He deserved that slap. And probably more.

She stepped toward the bedroom door, which was slightly ajar. She peered through the crack but couldn't see him, so she inched closer.

She heard a rustling noise and stepped back slightly. She could still see into the bedroom. He walked past the open door, and she caught a glimpse of his shirtless body.

His chest looked just as muscular as it felt when she had been pressed up against him earlier.

She bit her lip and shifted slightly so she could still see him. He walked to the closet and rummaged through his suitcase.

She really did pick the right man for the weekend, at least in terms of looks. Ethan didn't look nearly as good without his shirt on.

She needed to stop comparing every man she met to Ethan. She needed to move on. He definitely had. Ethan probably never thought about her anymore. Never wondered where things had gone wrong. Never laid in bed until the early morning hours, trying to figure out what he could have done differently to keep her interest.

He never had to wonder if he would ever be enough for anyone.

A sound from the bedroom caught her attention. She looked back through the crack in the door and drew in a sharp breath. He still had his back to her. Even from this angle, he looked good. Too good.

If she wasn't enough to keep the attention of someone like Ethan, there was no way she'd ever keep Bill's attention.

She turned around and surveyed the room. She cleaned up the remaining mess from their late-night supper and checked the lock on the door leading to the hallway.

Bill was still in the bedroom.

She glanced around the room again. They never discussed sleeping arrangements, and the hotel room only had one bed. Bill had brought her suitcase into the bedroom earlier, so maybe he assumed she would sleep in there and he'd sleep on the couch? But he went into the bedroom, so maybe he assumes that she'd sleep on the couch? It wasn't the 17th century, after all. Men didn't have to be chivalrous. She could sleep on the couch.

But she still wore the bathrobe, and her suitcase was in the bedroom. She couldn't go to sleep on the couch in the bathrobe. There was no guarantee that it would remain tied all night. The last thing she wanted was to wake up in the morning, naked, in front of a practical stranger.

That meant she had to go in the bedroom to get her suitcase.

She rolled her shoulders back, tightened the ties on her robe, and walked into the bedroom without knocking.

She quickly realized that she hadn't needed to enter so boldly. The bathroom door was closed tightly and the shower was running.

She sighed and turned to her suitcase. It was on the floor, next to the closet. She put on her pajamas and then surveyed herself in the mirror. Her eyes were still puffy from crying, but she looked alright overall. Her pajama shirt and shorts still felt new.

A noise came from the bathroom and she turned around just in time to see Bill step through the doorway. At least he wore boxers.

No shirt, though. Her heart skipped a beat. Sure, she caught a glimpse of his upper body just a few minutes ago, but that was through a crack in the door. Now that she saw him up close . . . even his abs had abs.

He walked into the room, right towards her. She shuffled sideways, but he didn't stop until he was right next to her. She glanced over. Of course, he was getting something out of his suitcase.

Emily let out a sigh of relief when he slid a t-shirt on.

He cleared his throat. "Do you realize that you slapped me when I looked at you that way?"

Busted. He definitely heard her sigh. "I wasn't looking at you in any way."

"Doesn't matter. Feel free to look."

"Are you really that full of yourself?"

He just shrugged and didn't say anything else before walking out of the bedroom.

Emily grabbed her toiletry bag from her suitcase and stomped to the bathroom. After a few minutes, she came out. The night had caught up with her, and she just wanted to be in bed, asleep. With any luck, she wouldn't dream that recurrent nightmare of Ethan cheating on her all over again.

He still was in the other room. That meant she could take the bed, right? If he wanted it, he should have claimed it first. She walked to the king-sized bed, pulled back the covers, and fluffed the pillow a few times. The bed was even more comfortable than she thought it would be. She reached over and flipped off the lamp on the nightstand.

Bill chose that moment to walk back into the room. Emily squeezed her eyes shut. He booked the hotel room himself, had insisted on doing that. The room only had one bed. Possession was nine-tenths of the law, right? Besides, what self-respecting person would wake up a sleeping individual only to kick them out of bed?

The other side of the bed sagged. She held her breath. Without looking, she could only guess at what he was doing over there. It sounded like he was moving around the extra pillows she had put on that half of the bed. Hotels always put too many pillows on the bed. Did he not realize that she put the pillows there to keep him away?

She couldn't even crack open one eye to spy on him since her back was to that side of the bed. But the mattress sagged again.

She stiffened. No, he wouldn't do that. He wouldn't.

He did. He got into the bed and was lying next to her. Not touching her in any way, but much too close for comfort.

She rolled over and opened her eyes. "What are you doing?"

He was on his back, staring at the dark ceiling. "Going to sleep. What are you doing?"

"I thought you were going to sleep on the couch. Isn't that why you left the room?"

"I left the room to check the door lock."

"You think I don't know how to lock a door by myself?"

He shifted slightly and looked directly at her. "Call it a personal quirk. I always check the locks myself. Like to know the room is secure."

She narrowed her eyes. "You really have a thing about security, don't you? You got a room on a floor that can only be accessed by a private elevator, inspected every window in this room as soon as we entered, and you checked the locks several times. Are you trying to avoid the mafia or something? Is someone trying to kill you?"

She meant that as a joke but she felt him stiffen beside her. "I thought you were tired."

"I am."

"So let's go to sleep."

"I thought you'd sleep on the couch."

"Did you see the size of that thing? I'm surprised you can even call it a couch."

She didn't want to say it, but he was right. "You booked the room. You could have booked one with two beds."

"I tried."

"Obviously not hard enough." She couldn't help it as the words flew out of her mouth.

He didn't say anything.

She took a deep breath in. "Look, I'm sorry. I didn't mean to be rude. It's been a long day." She rolled over to her side, facing him. "If you want, I can sleep on the—ouch!" She sat up and reached to her neck. Something sharp had scratched her.

"What's wrong?" He sat up and turned on the lamp on his side of the bed.

She blinked in the light. "Oh, nothing." She shifted slightly to hide the tag that was still attached to her pajamas.

He frowned and leaned over, tilting his head. "Is there something wrong with the pillows?" He lifted her pillow and ran his hand over the mattress, obviously looking for whatever poked her.

She sighed. If she knew anything about him at all after spending the last several hours together, it was that he was persistent in finding answers. If she wanted to go to sleep anytime soon, she needed to just tell him. "It was nothing really, just the price tag from my pajamas."

He stopped examining her pillow and looked at her. "You don't take the tags off your pajamas?"

She felt her face growing red. "They're new. I just bought them and forgot to take off the tag. It happens. No big deal."

A slow grin spread across his face. "You bought pajamas to impress me?"

That grin was dangerous. She grabbed an extra pillow and whacked him in the face. "No. I just didn't have pajamas to wear."

"Do you sleep naked?"

She whacked him again. This time, he caught the pillow before she made contact with his face. "I do not sleep naked. It's just that . . . well . . ." She was too tired to make up any excuses. She looked at him but couldn't hold his gaze, so she looked at the blanket. This was going to be embarrassing. "It was time for a change, you know? I used to sleep in Ethan's t-shirts because they smelled like him. I slept in them for two years. Then we broke up. For the past four months, I tried different styles of pajamas. Nothing felt right. I saw these in the store the other day and thought that maybe this style would feel right."

"Hmm." He didn't say anything, but she could feel his gaze on her.

"It's just that the nighttime can feel really lonely. I'm usually ok during the day. I stay focused on work and other activities. But at night, I'm all alone and sometimes . . . sometimes my mind just takes over, and it's hard to stop thinking about things." She grabbed a pillow and hugged it tightly.

He didn't say anything, so she risked glancing at him. He looked serious, like he was lost in his own thoughts. After a few seconds, he looked up at her. She shrugged. "Anyway, we should go to sleep. I can sleep on the couch." She turned to get out of bed but stopped when his hand landed gently on her shoulder.

"You don't have to go anywhere."

"I don't want you to feel sorry for me. I shouldn't have said any of that. I'm just tired." She turned again and stood up. "I'll be in the other room. Good night."

"Stop." His voice sounded different, deeper. She turned to look at him. He ran his hand through his hair. "I don't feel sorry for you. In fact, I know exactly how you feel." She raised an eyebrow at him and he held up a hand. "Ok, not exactly, but I know what it feels like to lie awake at night, alone with your darkest thoughts and fears. Trust me, things will get better."

She studied his face for a moment. He looked sincere. Then she remembered something he'd said before. "Oh right, I forgot that someone cheated on you before."

He shook his head. "No. I mean, yes. Yes, I had a girlfriend cheat on me. But that's not what keeps me up at night."

She chewed her lip. She didn't want to push him too far, but she wanted to know more about him. "What keeps you awake?"

His face darkened slightly. "I've just been through some things. Seen some things. But I promise you—" he looked at her with such intensity that she drew in a sharp breath "—things will get better. You'll find the comfortable pajamas."

She started to smile, but it turned into a yawn.

He patted the bed. "Come on. There's no point in either of us sleeping on that mini couch. I promise I'll be a gentleman."

She slowly got back into the bed, deliberately placing a pillow in the space between them.

"Good night, Bill."

"Good night, Emily." He turned off the lamp next to his side.

She turned over a few times, settling into the bed. Just when she stopped, Bill's voice broke through the night.

"You can borrow my t-shirt if you want something different to sleep in."

She grabbed the pillow from under her head and whacked him in the face. Judging by the sound that came from him, he never saw the attack coming.

She stifled her laugh. "Good night, Bill."

15

BILL

Bill squinted. The morning light shone through the partially open draperies on the hotel window. He closed those drapes last night. They shouldn't be open. He bolted out of bed, feet hitting the cold floor and hands raised in a fighting stance.

He caught a glimpse of motion by the door leading to the outer room of their hotel suite. He immediately turned in that direction, holding his breath while his heart pounded in his ears.

Within seconds, the door opened further and Emily stepped through, her gaze fixed on the two cups of coffee in her hands.

She gave him a quick glance before scanning the room. "Good, you're awake. I wasn't sure I should wake you or not, but I guess I don't need to worry about that. I brought you coffee from the lobby. No sugar this time." She kept walking as she talked until she reached the dresser and placed the cups of coffee on its top. Then she turned and looked at him. She took a step back. "Everything ok? Why are you standing like that?"

He glanced down. He didn't even realize his hands were

still raised in a fighting stance. Freakin' PTSD. As if what he'd been through in the military wasn't enough, he also had to face the awkward questions about the weird things he did now.

He pasted on a charming grin. Most women liked that grin. He took a few jabs in the air as he fixed his eyes on her. "Don't you ever work out in the morning? You should really try it. Just five minutes of kickboxing will really get you moving for the day. Works almost as well as coffee." He threw a few more deliberate punches for show and then stood up straight. "No sugar?"

"Just cream. I promise." She held up her right hand.

"Hmm, what did I do to deserve such special treatment?" He walked closer to her until he could reach his coffee. He took a sip without breaking eye contact with her. It burned his tongue but that didn't matter. Judging by the expression on her face, she forgot all about his fighting stance from just a few seconds ago.

"I figured that I should keep you happy today since you are playing the role of a lifetime this afternoon," she said.

He raised his eyebrow and enjoyed watching her cheeks turn slightly red.

"Thanks." He walked past her to his suitcase, grabbed some clothes, and went into the bathroom, closing the door behind him.

A few minutes later, he walked back out into the outer room of their suite. He hadn't really taken the time to notice the luxury in the suite last night. The kitchenette had white counters, possibly quartz, and the floor was hardwood. He always liked hotels with wood floors. Hotel carpeting just never felt or looked very clean. The separate seating area hosted a widescreen TV and two small sofas, which were more the size of overstuffed armchairs than couches. A sliding glass door led to a small balcony, where Emily sat.

He opened the glass door and walked out to the balcony to join Emily. No wonder she chose to drink her coffee out here. The weather was mildly brisk, there wasn't a cloud in the sky, and the lake shimmered from this view.

He could spend an entire day looking at the lake or, better yet, hiking around the surrounding woods. Nothing made him feel more at peace than a day spent in nature.

He sat in the empty chair next to Emily. "Mind if I join you?"

She smiled. "Not at all. I thought I'd drink my coffee out here and read."

He glanced at his watch. "It's almost nine."

"I know."

"Do you need to get ready?"

She shrugged. "The wedding isn't for another few hours. It doesn't take me that long to get ready." She rolled her eyes at him in a playful manner. "What are your plans this morning? Didn't you say that you were going somewhere this morning?"

"Did you forget about the spa?"

"No, I didn't. I ate breakfast when I picked up the coffee. I'm going to relax, then watch a movie and paint my nails. You know, so no one will realize that I didn't actually get a professional manicure and pedicure." She examined her nails as she spoke.

He watched her, amused. "Suit yourself. I'll call down to cancel your spa package. At this point, they'll probably charge me the full price anyway. But it's your choice. Go or don't go."

Her eyes widened. "Wait . . . do you mean that you actually booked me a spa package?"

He stood up and stared out at the lake. It really was a beautiful view.

"You know that wasn't necessary."

"Very few things are necessary. But they can still be fun." He took a deep breath in, letting the morning lake air fill his lungs.

"Well, I'm going to pay for it. And the room."

He was glad that his back was to her so he didn't have to mask the look on his face. "I can afford it. Consider it a peace offering for making you car sick yesterday. Or for the thing I said before you, well, you know." He rubbed the spot on his cheek where she had slapped him.

"Well, I don't know . . ."

He turned around and stared at her. Why was she so stubborn? And why did he like it so much?

"Let me at least pay for dinner tonight," she said.

He couldn't help but grin at her determination. "Don't tell me that we'll have to pay for our own food at the wedding reception?"

She blushed. "Well, no, I guess not. I'll take you out to dinner next weekend."

"Are you asking me out on a date?" He couldn't help himself from asking. He liked watching her blush.

"No. Just as friends. We can go out with Ashley and Michael."

"Double date?"

She shook her head even faster. "No . . . I mean . . ."

She was obviously flustered. Bill took pity on her. "I'd love to go out with you sometime. But I can't next weekend." Or any weekend. Or any weekday, either, once he moved back to his parents' house. But he didn't want to think about that yet.

He glanced at his watch again. "The spa is waiting for you. You can still be on time if you leave now."

"Ok. What are you going to do this morning?"

"Just some things." He didn't need to tell her about his planned visit to his parents' house. No need to share the more painful details of life with her. Their relationship was surface-level and fake. That's how it needed to stay. "I'll be back in time to get ready for the wedding."

She tilted her head and bit her lip. She stood up hesitantly and then took a quick step towards him. Before he realized what she was doing, she wrapped her arms around him in a hug. He inhaled sharply. Her hair smelled just as captivating as the night before. He wrapped his arms around her tightly in return.

Without a word, she broke away from their hug just as quickly as she had started it and walked away.

BILL

Bill sat in the driveway, staring at the house in front of him. His childhood home. It looked the same but different. The home of his childhood had been meticulously maintained. The house now obviously needed some attention.

The front lawn was neatly mowed. His father used to take great pride in maintaining a neat yard. But one day, his dad got confused when trying to turn on the mower. Bill sold the mower the next time he visited and hired a lawn service instead.

The shutters surrounding the windows on the two-story building could use a fresh coat of paint. The front porch needed paint too, and he couldn't remember if the rain gutters were cleaned last fall. Probably wouldn't hurt to call a company and get them cleaned again.

He grabbed his phone and jotted down a few reminders. He could make most of the calls this week and inspect the work next weekend. But that meant he'd also need to check on Julie's schedule and see if she could be at the house when the work was scheduled. Last time a roof inspector had come, his father, William, was in the middle of a bad day and chased him off the property before calling the police.

Maybe Julie really was right. He needed to be here to help. He should have moved back months ago.

He got out of the car as another vehicle pulled into the driveway. He waited until Julie parked and got out, then he walked over and gave her a hug before glancing into her backseat.

"Where's John?"

"Hello to you, too." She gave him a playful punch in the shoulder. "He's at a friend's house. They invited him to the playground this morning. He made me promise that I'd take care of Boo Boo the Second until he got home."

A sinking feeling came over Bill and he slapped his forehead. "Boo Boo . . . I'm so sorry, Jules. I—"

"Don't tell me you forgot to get him the fish! You promised him!"

"No, I remembered. I just left it at the hotel this morning." He could clearly see the fish's location on the hotel kitchen counter in his mind's eye. "Can you come by and pick it up this afternoon?"

"No, I'm too busy. Can you bring it here this afternoon?"

"I have that wedding to get to."

"Fine. I'll tell John that you'll bring Boo Boo the next time you're here. When's that?"

"I'll be back Friday. But I can't make him wait that long." A week might as well be a year in the mind of a four-year-old. "I'll bring it by tomorrow morning before I head back to the city."

Julie let out a sigh of relief. "You're the best. Thanks, big bro."

"Anytime, little sis." She meant well. He knew she did. So the guilt washed over him. A good brother would never have expected her to take on the care of their parents while being a single mother, with only some weekend help from him.

"Before we go inside, I have something to tell you." He took a deep inhale. It would be like ripping off a bandaid. The faster he said it, the less it would hurt. "I talked with the chief of staff at Clareville County Hospital. They offered me a job, and I signed the contract a few days ago. If all goes well, I can move here in about a month."

He was wrong. Saying the words quickly still hurt. But Julie's reaction helped. Her mouth dropped open, and she grasped him in a hug.

"Did they decide that they need a cardiologist here in town? Are you going to start a cardiology unit at the hospital?"

Bill tried to hide his disappointment. The town's hospital could barely be called a hospital. It was small, with an emergency department and one small inpatient ward. Most surgical patients were transferred to larger hospitals in the closest city, about sixty miles away. Same with the more severe emergencies.

"No, but they do need a general practitioner."

"Well, that's great news. I can't tell you how relieved I'll be once you're here."

He pulled back from her hug as he heard the front door open, followed by his father's voice, yelling something indecipherable.

He glanced up to the front door where his father stood in the opening, hair askew and a bathrobe wrapped around his body. The bottom half of his jeans appeared under the bathrobe, and he wore one slipper and one boot.

"Looks like he's not having a great day." He didn't want to look at Julie when he spoke.

"No, he isn't. Dementia can kiss my—"

"I agree." He interrupted her. "Let's go inside."

17

EMILY

Emily exited the spa more relaxed than she had imagined possible. Even on a regular day, she never felt this relaxed. Bill really knew how to be a good boyfriend.

Pretend boyfriend.

Temporary boyfriend.

Players were dangerous, and she needed to remember that. Even Ashley didn't deny that Bill was a player. Bill was only here for the wedding, and then she'd stay away from him. She wasn't going to repeat the same mistake she made when she dated Ethan. She learned her lesson the first time.

However, how often did a man come along and surprise a woman with a morning at the spa during their first official date, hours before attending the wedding of her ex-fiancé?

She felt so relaxed that she actually smiled at Ethan and his mom when she passed them in the hotel lobby. His mother stopped and stared. Ethan looked like he'd swallowed a toad.

"Emily, how nice to see you." Ethan's mother, Deborah, eyed her suspiciously.

"Hello Deborah, Ethan." What was in that massage lotion?

She didn't have that familiar urge to vomit from seeing either of them.

"Emily, it's been a while. Didn't think you'd make it here." Ethan's face looked strained. Fine by her. It was his own fault that she was at his wedding. He chose to have an affair with her cousin.

"It's my cousin's wedding. Of course, I would come. I'm not going to turn my back on my family." Or endure the unending comments from some of the gossipy family members.

"I hope you won't make a scene at the ceremony," said Deborah.

She considered her response carefully. She didn't want to lose that Zen feeling. "I have no intentions of doing anything other than having a good time."

He crossed his arms and looked at his mother. "Mom, can I talk with Emily alone for a minute?"

Deborah looked less than excited about that idea. She always liked to control Ethan. "Do you really think that is a good idea? You are about to get married." She half-whispered the words in a fake attempt to be discreet, but obviously, she wanted Emily to hear everything. "You never know what—" she tilted her head in Emily's direction "—might say to mess things up. She was always a bit territorial."

Emily rolled her eyes openly. "You have nothing to worry about. In case you didn't notice, I'm here with my boyfriend."

Deborah turned back to Emily as if she was surprised to hear her speak. "Oh, right. Your date. Is he a family friend? So nice that you could find someone to come with you." Her voice dripped with false sweetness.

The hairs on the back of Emily's neck started to rise. Emily turned back to Ethan. "If there's anything else you wanted to discuss, we need to do it quickly. My morning appointment ran late and I should get back to my room."

"Hmph." Deborah didn't even try to hide her disapproval. "So it's true? I couldn't even believe it when I heard that you refused to help your cousin this morning. She was really counting on you to get them anything they needed. She and her entire bridal party had to order room service because you weren't there to get them coffee."

"My boyfriend surprised me with a spa morning. If she wanted my help, she could have asked me earlier in the week."

"*Tsk tsk.* Everyone knows that the bride comes first on her wedding day."

Emily took a slow inhale. "I really have to go. I'm sure I'll see both of you later." She turned around and walked straight to the elevator.

This actually felt good. A week ago, a conversation like this could have destroyed her. Made her cry, or at least sent her to the grocery store for large amounts of ice cream.

But she felt nothing when she saw Ethan today.

His mother was another story. She had at least been cordial to her in the past. But apparently, Deborah no longer felt the need to be even slightly polite.

She almost made it to the elevator before Ethan's voice cut through her thoughts.

"Emily, wait up a minute."

Emily stopped about ten feet from the elevator. Even if she ran, the elevator door wouldn't open before he caught up. She might as well face him straight on.

She turned around. He was even closer than she expected. He grabbed her upper arm and forcefully motioned toward a pair of chairs in a corner of the lobby.

"Let go." Emily pulled her arm but he held on. "Don't touch me!"

"Don't make a scene, Emily." He glared at her but let go. "Let's go talk somewhere private."

"I'm not going anywhere with you. What do you want?" She crossed her arms and remained firmly planted.

"Seriously? That's how you are going to play this? Like you don't know what the problem is?" His eyes got that familiar glint that she only recently realized meant that he was trying to blame her for things that weren't her fault.

"Ethan, I'm just here to see my cousin get married. Leave me alone."

"You are planning something." His eyes narrowed with the accusation.

Emily's brain started to whirl. "I'm planning nothing at all. I would never intentionally hurt someone else. Even you."

"If you weren't planning something, you wouldn't have brought Bill." He practically spat the words.

"Bill is my date. I didn't even know that he knew you until last night."

"You knew exactly what you were doing." He put his hand to his forehead and shook his head slowly, letting out a low chuckle. "All the time we dated, you hid your true nature so well. You fooled me. I never realized you could be so manipulative and vindictive."

Emily's face grew hot and her jaw tensed. How could she have ever loved him? No one had ever called her those things before. She wasn't perfect, and she wasn't a saint, but she never tried to hurt anyone, ever. Not intentionally.

"Ethan, I have to go."

"Not before you tell me why you brought Bill."

"I brought him as my date. End of story."

"You are either lying or you're just really stupid. How did you find out?" His face was red, and she could tell he was trying not to yell.

"Find out what?"

"That he was one of the guys who got me kicked out of the Army!"

She blinked. What did he mean? "He was in the Army?"

He watched her reaction carefully. "You didn't know? You aren't dating him, are you? That's the sort of thing that anyone would know about their boyfriend."

"Umm, well, I guess we just never really talked about that. But that doesn't matter. We talk about a lot of other things."

"He probably never told you because he's an embarrassment to the Army. He should have been kicked out, not me." He shifted his weight angrily. "Remember how I told you about what happened when I was deployed? His unit was already there. He was a medic. I met him on the first or second day there. Thought he was cool for the first few weeks. But then he testified against me after it all happened, and I got kicked out."

"Are you talking about the time you got written up for returning to base after curfew?"

He sneered condescendingly. "You don't get written up for being out past curfew when you're deployed. Where did you think I'd go? Out to a bar? That was during basic training, and they have too many rules during basic training."

"Then what are you talking about?"

"Jeez, it's like you never listened to me when I talked. I'm talking about the time we were busted for gambling. He was jealous that I didn't let him in on a deal I made with some of the other guys."

"You and Bill gambled when you were deployed?" Emily tried to picture Bill doing something like that and failed. She couldn't even picture him deployed or in the military.

"It wasn't gambling. Just placing small bets on things."

"What types of things?"

"The usual. Sports, mostly. That doesn't matter. Listen, the point is he turned me in, and you brought him here to ruin the wedding."

"Isn't gambling legal in some places?"

"Of course you wouldn't understand." Ethan's voice turned sour. "You can't run a gambling ring when you are deployed. That's illegal."

Emily tried not to roll her eyes. If anyone needed an example of how man-splaining sounded, a two-minute conversation with Ethan would provide the perfect example.

"I even offered him a deal. He could have won a lot of money. Instead, he turned me in and even testified against me during the trial."

"Am I really hearing this correctly? You are mad at *Bill*, because he turned you in for operating an illegal gambling ring?"

"There's supposed to be a military code of honor. You don't tattle on your buddy."

"I would think it's more important to follow the law."

"And that's why we aren't together anymore."

She felt sick to her stomach. Even after all this time apart, more and more of his secrets and lies were finding their way to the surface. And worst of all, he never took responsibility for his actions. "Ethan, I have to go."

He looked at her, his eyes hard and cold. "He messed up my life once. He's your guest today. Make sure he doesn't do anything stupid." He didn't even wait for an answer. He just turned around and started walking away.

Emily stared after him for a moment before the guilt started tearing away at her insides.

"Ethan, wait!"

He turned around and looked at her, eyes still cold. She took a few steps towards him, then stopped.

"Look, I just want to know . . . I mean, Veronica is my cousin and my family. I need to know that you really love her. That you'll treat her right."

"We're getting married in a few hours."

She shook her head and took another step towards him.

"That's not what I'm asking. I need to know that you are the right person for Veronica. I don't want her to go through heartbreak. I don't want you to hurt her. I want her to be happy. And if being with you makes her happy, then I want you to be happy too."

"What are you doing, Emily? You have really bad timing."

"Bad timing?"

"You and I are over. Don't mess things up today just because you are bitter. You'll only end up embarrassing yourself."

"I'm not trying to do anything. I just want to know that—"

He leaned forward. She automatically stepped back. The vein on his forehead was starting to pop out, the same way it always did when he got mad.

He lowered his voice to a hiss. "Why did you even come here? You aren't welcome. I don't want you here. I don't want Bill here. And if you think you are going to ruin this wedding, you are even more pathetic and—"

"You better stop right there. I'm not trying to ruin anything."

"Does Bill know how selfish you are? Or how—?" He stopped talking suddenly, his face going pale like he'd seen a ghost.

A familiar deep voice came from behind Emily. "Am I interrupting something?"

Emily didn't need to turn around to know Bill was there. She spoke without turning around. "Ethan decided that we aren't welcome here."

"Does that mean we're skipping the wedding?"

Emily paused as Bill wrapped his arm around her shoulder so they were standing side by side, facing Ethan. "I guess so. He made it pretty clear that we aren't invited." Emily tried to ignore the sting she felt over being uninvited to her own family's gathering. As much as she dreaded going to the wedding, it felt a thousand times worse to be actively excluded.

Bill spoke again. "We don't have to go. We can find other things to do." He pulled Emily in possessively.

Ethan scowled and pointed his finger at Emily. "You manipulative little—" Emily felt Bill pull away from her slightly. Ethan must have noticed the same because he paused briefly. "If you skip the wedding now, everyone is going to feel bad for you. No one will care about our wedding. You have to come."

"I put up with a lot of things when we were together. But you have no right to treat me like this. Bill, let's go." She started to turn.

Ethan reached out and grabbed her free arm. "Wait!"

She pulled back. "Don't touch me, Ethan."

Bill stepped forward, releasing his grasp around Emily's shoulders. He partially blocked her view of Ethan. When he spoke, his voice was low and deep. "Let's get one thing straight, Ethan. Emily is with me. You will treat her with respect. And you won't touch her again."

Ethan took a step towards Bill, puffing his chest. A thin line of sweat across his forehead betrayed his confidence. "If she doesn't go to the wedding, I'll tell everyone that it's because she begged me to run away with her this morning."

"Why would she possibly want to run away with you when everyone knows that she's here with me?"

"Are you saying that you are better than me?"

"You said it. I didn't."

"Guys, enough." Emily looked back and forth between the two men as she spoke.

She may as well have saved her breath. Bill looked at her and nodded, but Ethan ignored her.

"She has to be at the wedding." Ethan pointed at Emily

and stepped closer again. Bill reacted, stepping between them.

"Back away from Emily." From the tone of his voice, Bill meant business.

"Tell her to go to the wedding." Ethan's voice rose.

Emily put her hand on Bill's back and stepped so she was next to him again. This time, Ethan looked at her while Bill kept his gaze fixed on Ethan. "Ethan, stop. I came here for the wedding. Then you told me I wasn't welcome. Now you are blackmailing me to make sure I'm there. What do you want?"

He let out an exasperated sigh. "Veronica wants you there. She's your cousin. She actually feels bad about how things happened. And to answer your question from earlier . . ." He glanced at Bill before continuing. "I do. I love her, and I will never hurt her."

Emily glared at him. "What will happen when you get bored with her and notice someone else? Are you going to cheat on her, like you cheated on me?"

"Never. She's everything to me. I'm going to marry her, and I'm going to mean every word I say during the ceremony. I can't live without her."

Emily felt the block of ice within her heart start to melt slowly. She still hated Ethan and didn't want to be near him for a second longer than necessary, but maybe she'd be able to forgive him someday. Or at least stop worrying that Veronica was making the biggest mistake of her life.

Maybe Ethan did have a connection with Veronica that was better than anything they'd ever had together.

"Come to the wedding," Ethan said. "Please."

18

EMILY

"Bill, let's go." She motioned toward the elevator and started walking. Bill waited for a second, then easily caught up with her with several long steps.

She stabbed the button for the elevator with her finger. Thankfully, it opened immediately. She stepped inside and barely waited for Bill to follow before pressing the button for their floor.

The doors closed, and Emily stood, facing the front without looking behind her.

But the doors opened again, revealing the same lobby.

"What the heck?" she muttered and stabbed the button for floor ten again. The stupid elevator doors remained open, so she started hitting buttons at random. If the doors didn't close soon and take her away from the elevator lobby, she was going to lose it.

At least Ethan wasn't seeing this. She caught a last glance of his back as he went around a corner on the other side of the lobby.

But his mother was still in the lobby, by the concierge desk. And she was watching.

Emily stabbed the button one more time. Her face burned hotter than it had felt in months. Maybe even as bad as when she finally realized the extent of Ethan's betrayal.

The door didn't close.

"Forget this. I'm taking the stairs." She didn't even turn around to look at Bill. He could choose to take the stairs, too, or wait forever in the broken elevator. Didn't matter to her. If she didn't get somewhere private fast, she was going to explode. And not in a good way.

"Wait." Bill stepped next to her and waved his room key in front of a sensor above the buttons on the elevator panel. "Sorry, it took me a minute to find the key."

The elevator door closed as soon as he pressed the button, just as Emily noticed Ethan's mother giving her an obvious smirk.

That woman never liked her. Emily never understood why.

The elevator rose to their floor in silence. When it stopped and the doors opened, Emily walked out and headed straight for their room. She reached the door and started fumbling in her pockets for the room key.

Bill caught up with her again, but she didn't look at him. The key had to be in one of her pockets. Unless she left it in the spa. Or did she even bring it with her?

Just like in the elevator, Bill reached around her and waved the room card in front of the sensor and opened the door.

She walked in and sighed. Finally, she was somewhere private, somewhere where she wouldn't run into Ethan or his family.

Now she just had to figure out how to deal with Bill. She didn't want to have a crying session in front of him again. Not over Ethan. She did not want him to think that she was crying over that man.

Because she wasn't. Marrying Ethan would have been the worst mistake of her life. She deserved better than him.

Her phone dinged, so she pulled it out of her pocket and then groaned. There were three missed texts from Ashley, one from Theresa, and a new text that just came in from Ethan.

She raised her hand to throw her phone when Bill stepped up behind her and wrapped his arms around her with her back pressed to his chest.

"You'll only regret breaking your phone if you throw it." His voice was low and steady.

"You don't know that."

"I do. I speak from experience."

She closed her eyes and focused on the feel of his body pressed up against her back. Her body relaxed against his.

"Let me take a guess. Ethan texted you?"

She let herself enjoy one more second of his embrace before she pulled away. She walked to the couch, patting the cushion next to her, inviting him to join her. She didn't realize how small the couch was until he sat next to her. There was no way for them to both sit on the couch without their legs touching.

"He had the guts to ask again if I'm still going to the wedding." She held the phone out to Bill.

"Why didn't you block his number months ago?"

"This whole situation is embarrassing. I'm really sorry that you had to witness that conversation between us in the lobby. He acted differently when we dated."

Bill looked at her closely. "You don't need to explain anything to me."

"But I do. I don't want you to think that I'm a person who is willing to stay in a relationship with someone who treated me so badly. He was good to me, most of the time." She bit her lip. Now that she said the words out loud, she wasn't so confident that they were true. "Besides the cheating and the lying, he acted like he liked me. I mean, loved me."

She watched as Bill's face softened. "I met Ethan a long time ago. He turned out to be one of the most manipulative people I know," he said.

She looked at his message on her phone again. "I guess I should text him back."

"What's the plan? Are we going or not?"

"I hate to say it, but I need to go. I can't let him chase me away from my own family."

Bill stood up. "Then let's go. Do you want to shower first, or should I?" He motioned to the bathroom.

"Wait. Don't you think we should warn Veronica first? I mean, she's about to marry a master manipulator. This could be the worst decision of her life."

"If you try to warn her now, you'll play into his game. Didn't you hear him in the lobby? He won't hesitate to tell your family that your plan is to win him back."

Her stomach dropped. "So you think I should just let my cousin marry him without telling her how horrible he is?"

He nodded. "She already knows. She dated him, fully aware that he was engaged to you. She knows who she is marrying."

She frowned. "But still, shouldn't I try to warn her?"

He sat down again next to her. "I'm never going to tell you what to do. But I don't think it's a good idea. It's too late to say anything to her."

Emily considered his words before she responded. "The wedding is only a few hours away. I doubt I could even get a minute alone with her. And, I think I believe him when he says he loves her." She sighed. "We probably should get ready. Mind if I shower first?"

He patted her leg. "Go ahead."

She grabbed her phone and walked to the bathroom. Bill

had surprised her in the past few minutes. He listened to her and gave her good advice, something Ethan had never done. Actually, he also listened last night when she cried. He even stood up for her in the lobby. She definitely didn't need a man to come in and save her, but still, she liked the way he defended and supported her. Maybe there was more to him than she thought. Maybe he wasn't just a playboy. Maybe . . .

She needed a hot shower to clear her head. She turned on the shower water and picked up her phone to text Ethan back. She would let him know that she was still coming and then block his number from her phone.

The only problem was, the phone she grabbed from the living room looked like hers but wasn't. Bill's phone, with its remarkably similar case, was in her hand. And there was a text on the screen from a woman named Meredith.

I made the reservations for dinner next Saturday night. Can't wait to see you! xoxo

19

EMILY

Two days, and two texts from two different women.

At least, two texts that she knew of. It was really none of her business, anyway. She wasn't really his girlfriend. They weren't really dating. Their entire relationship revolved around this weekend. He only agreed to date her as a favor. Once the weekend ended, their relationship ended.

If she had any common sense, she'd remember that. Their relationship wasn't going to last beyond the weekend.

There was no chance that the two of them would end up together. She needed to forget how ridiculously attractive he was. And how he stood up for her in front of Ethan. And booked them a room on a private floor of the hotel so the room was a private escape, with no chance that Veronica, Ethan, or any member of Ethan's family could stop by the room. And he treated her to a morning at the spa.

No, he would be nothing but heartbreak. Once a player, always a player.

She took a quick shower and walked back into the room. Bill was still where she left him, relaxing on the couch in the outer room of their suite. The open balcony doors allowed a warm breeze to enter the room. She wrapped her towel around her tighter.

She cleared her throat and Bill looked up at her. "Um, here's your phone. You got a text. I didn't mean to read it. I thought it was my phone. I guess we have similar cases." She held the phone out to him and he took it.

"Thanks." He didn't even look at the phone before putting it in his pocket.

That was annoying. She wanted to see his face when he read the text. Would he be excited that Meredith had reservations? He'd probably gone on at least one date with Meredith already. He seemed like the kind of guy who would plan a first date himself. Plus, they must have talked about where they would go since she didn't mention the name of a restaurant in the text.

She shook her head. His business was his own private business. Not hers. She didn't need to turn into a jealous woman just because Ethan broke her trust time and time again.

Bill could date whomever he wanted.

Actually . . . she could also date whomever she wanted.

It was time to move on. It was time to date someone else.

Bill stood up, and Emily realized that she still stood in the middle of the room. He looked at her expectantly.

"We, well, we don't have too much time to get ready. You can have the bathroom, but I need to change. So go now, but do me a favor and don't come out of the bathroom until I'm all done changing."

He nodded. "Fine." He brushed past her and, moments later, she heard the click of the bathroom door closing.

She followed him into the bedroom and then waited a few seconds until the shower turned on. This was her chance.

She grabbed her phone and dialed Ashley.

"Hey Ash, I only have a few minutes. But I need to talk with you."

"Sure. What's up?" There was the sound of a man laughing in the background, possibly her boyfriend.

"Are you alone?"

"I'm with Michael. But I can be alone. Give me a minute." The sounds on the other end were muffled for a minute. Then Ashley spoke again. "I'm alone. What's going on? How are you and Bill getting along?"

"Fine. I mean, really good. But he just got another text from a different woman. This guy must date around like crazy." She glanced at the bathroom door. The shower was still running.

"Yeah, I told you that Michael said he dates a lot. But Michael also said he's a really good guy. Maybe he just needs to find the right woman before he settles down."

"I agree. But it's definitely not me."

"Why would you say that? Is he acting like a jerk or something?"

"No, he's fine. I just can't date a player. But guess who we ran into earlier?"

Ashley groaned. "Oh no, please don't tell me that you saw Ethan."

"Yup. Sometimes, I can't remember what I ever saw in him."

"So it's time to move on?"

"Definitely."

"Are you going to move on with Bill?" Ashley's voice rose as she spoke. "We could go on double dates together. It would be perfect!"

"Don't get excited! Definitely not him. I mean, he's pretty perfect, but he's a player. Remember that night we all met at the restaurant? And how I told you about when we met for coffee? He had to sit next to the wall the entire time so he could check out all the women in the room. I won't put up with cheating or anything close to it."

"That's so weird. There has to be an explanation for that. I can't believe Michael would be best friends with a guy who disrespects women like that."

Emily thought for a moment. Ashley's boyfriend, Michael, had always acted respectfully around them. Bill, on the other hand, confused her. He wasn't perfect, but he definitely seemed to be considerate. So why had he insisted on sitting against the wall in the restaurant and the café?

"So, what are you going to do instead?" Ashley's question brought her back out of her thoughts.

Emily took a deep breath. She was glad they were on the phone instead of video chatting or talking face-to-face. "I'm actually thinking about making a profile on a dating app."

"That sounds great! It's the perfect way to get back into the dating scene."

Emily opened her mouth to speak again but stopped when the shower water turned off. She lowered her voice into a whisper. "Listen, I have to go. Bill just got out of the shower. I'll call you tomorrow."

"Ok. Try to have fun at the reception! And don't do anything I wouldn't do!"

Emily hung up as Ashley laughed. She shook her head and walked over to the closet. Bill's voice came from the bathroom.

"Em, you dressed yet? I'm ready to come out."

She hadn't even started getting dressed yet. She flung open her suitcase. "I need a few more minutes."

"What if I come out and keep my eyes closed?"

She glared at the bathroom door. "Don't you dare. Besides, you'd run into everything if your eyes were closed."

"I could keep them open and just not look at you."

She paused. His voice sounded playful. Was he flirting? "Ha. I don't trust you enough for that."

"Well, it's not like I haven't seen you in a towel before."

Her heart skipped a beat. He definitely sounded like he was flirting. "Give me a minute and you can come out."

"I'll start counting now. One . . . two . . . three . . ."

Emily grabbed her bra and underwear from her suitcase and pulled the dress off the hanger. "I can't get dressed if you are counting so loud! And count slower!"

He started counting faster. "Twelve . . . thirteen . . . fourteen . . ."

"Don't you dare come out of that bathroom." She opened the package for her backless bra. How was she supposed to put it on? The thing came with directions. Seriously, it would take much longer than a minute just to read the directions, much less put on the bra.

"Fifty-five . . . fifty-six . . ."

"Bill . . ."

"Fifty-seven . . ."

She grabbed the bathrobe from the closet and threw it tightly around her, so she was covered by both the towel and the robe.

"Sixty."

Emily looked at the door. It was still firmly closed.

"Bill?"

"Emily?"

"Are you coming out?"

"Am I allowed?" he asked through the door.

"Yes. I'm wearing a robe."

She waited for the door to open, but there was only silence from the other room.

"Are you coming out?" she asked.

"I can't. I'm naked."

She stifled a laugh.

He continued. "Unlike you, I can't get fully dressed in a minute."

She rolled her eyes. He'd really sounded serious about only waiting a minute to come out. "Well, I'm going to need a few more minutes to get dressed."

"That's fine. I have my clothes in here with me."

She looked at the door. Was he purposefully trying to drive her crazy? "So you don't need to come out to get ready?"

"Nope. I just liked messing with you. You sound cute when you're flustered."

Her stomach fluttered. "I don't get flustered."

"Sure."

She looked at the instructions for her bra again. There were little stickers that had to be unpeeled from the sides of the cups. Ugh. She tentatively lifted the bra to compare it to the drawing in the instructions.

"Whatever you do, don't come out." She held her breath until she heard his reply.

"Take your time. I was just teasing you before."

She glanced at the bra again, then at the closet. The other dress she brought was much more conservative—it didn't require a backless bra. It looked more like something that she'd wear to a funeral than a wedding but was definitely a safer choice.

But she didn't want safe tonight. She wanted to look amazing.

She took a deep breath in and focused on getting into the backless bra. It stayed in place for a few seconds, so she stepped into the dress, wiggling until it fell into place. The bottom of her dress brushed her knee, with a small slit on one side. Dark purple lace layered the front, with a halter top tied behind her neck, exposing her entire back. The dress hugged all her curves and fit like a glove.

She stood in front of the mirror. This dress was different from her normal style. More revealing. But still classy.

She swallowed hard. She could still change into her other dress. It wasn't nearly as flattering and didn't show off her curves the way this one did. The other dress was a much safer option.

But . . . if she was really going to start dating again, she wanted to feel comfortable in her own skin. She hadn't even tried to feel attractive for months. This dress screamed confidence. This dress sent the message that the person wearing it believed in herself. This dress made a statement.

She wanted to be that confident woman again. She wanted to stand tall and be brave.

She was going to wear that dress. And she was going to wear it with the strappy, silver high heels Theresa insisted she buy.

Now she just needed to figure out her makeup.

She started rummaging through her bag when a noise from the bathroom distracted her.

Bill! She completely forgot that he remained trapped in the bathroom so she could get dressed.

She cleared her throat. "Bill? I'm dressed. You can come out if you want." She stood up tall, smoothing out the invisible wrinkles in her dress.

A second later, the bathroom door opened.

20

EMILY

His opinion of her dress really didn't matter. He could hate it and she would still wear it. She picked it out because she liked how it looked and how she felt in it. He didn't have to agree.

She studied his face as he walked out of the bathroom. He wore a light-blue dress shirt and black dress pants, but she spared only a quick glance at his clothes.

His eyes widened as he stared at her. He let out a low gasp as he ran his eyes up and down her dress. She fought the urge to shiver. His reaction really didn't matter to her.

He didn't break eye contact as he walked toward her. "You look . . ."

She bit her lip. He didn't finish his sentence. What was he thinking? She should have just worn the other dress. This dress was too much for the wedding. She wanted to look good, but not . . . well, not *too* good.

He walked up to her and held out his hand. She placed her hand in his, and he gave her a little tug before spinning her around once.

She stopped moving when she faced him again. He didn't let go of her hand.

"You look stunning."

Emily tried to keep her breathing steady. "I'm not ready yet. I haven't even put on my makeup."

"You don't need makeup to look good."

Emily felt the corners of her lips raise in a smile but couldn't really think about that. She needed to learn how to breathe again.

He let out a deep sigh and brushed back a piece of hair from her face. His hand paused briefly on the side of her neck.

When he spoke, his voice was husky. "I got you something to wear to the wedding. I hope I'm not being too presumptuous."

She shook her head. She couldn't find any words.

"Turn around."

She did as he asked. Was this going to be like a moment in the movies when the guy placed a beautiful necklace around the woman's neck? No, that was a ridiculous thought. Real guys, in her experience, weren't that romantic.

He stepped in close behind her, his breath gentle on her ear. He ran his hand through her hair, starting at the section right above her ear and brushing her hair away, leaving her neck exposed.

She couldn't help but shiver this time.

"Are you cold?"

"No, just not used to having my back exposed." She swallowed again, trying to sound convincing.

"Hold still for just a second."

She didn't move. He placed his hand on the side of her head again, gently tangling his fingers in her hair. She felt his other hand press something against the skin behind her ear.

Within a second, his hands fell away and released her from whatever spell he'd temporarily placed on her.

She whirled back around, placing her hand up to her ear instinctively. Something was there. A bandaid? Why would anyone put a bandaid on someone's head right before going to a wedding?

She opened her mouth to speak but he was faster. "You said you don't have any allergies, right? No bad reaction to medications? And you aren't on any medications right now?"

She shook her head as he spoke.

"No pre-existing health problems?" He studied her face closely.

"What are you talking about? I'm perfectly healthy, not that it's any of your concern." She walked to the full-length mirror on the closet door and angled her head to see the bandaid.

He followed her and stood behind her. He gently moved her hair aside so she could see her exposed ear better. "It's a patch for motion sickness. A prescription patch."

She narrowed her eyes.

"I called in a prescription for it and picked it up this morning while I was out."

She crossed her arms and said nothing.

"You looked like you were ready to knock on death's door after the car ride yesterday." His voice was barely above a whisper as he spoke, and he ran his finger over the patch behind her ear. "I couldn't watch you go through that again today."

She considered his words carefully.

He started to look guilty. "Shoot. You're mad. I'm sorry. I didn't even know if the pharmacy would have any in stock, and I didn't want to get your hopes up. I should have asked you first."

She raised her hand and placed it on his, which still rested on her upper neck. "I think—" she swallowed hard "—this might have been the most romantic thing anyone has done for me."

She turned around to face him, and he leaned down slightly, looking deep into her eyes. He slipped his hand around the back of her neck again. "If that's the most romantic thing anyone has done for you, then you better hold on tight."

"What?" Emily barely got the word out before Bill's lips reached hers. His lips were soft and gentle at first, moving slowly against hers.

She hesitated at first, then moved her lips in response. His hand moved against the back of her neck, drawing her closer.

She wanted to be close to him, wanted his body pressed up against hers. She wanted his arms wrapped around her, feeling captured in his embrace. She wanted to feel nothing but his lips against her lips.

She tried not to groan as he pulled back slightly; instead, she grabbed his shirt, pulling him back to her, not ready for the kiss to end.

If they were going to kiss, she wasn't going to stop until she was ready to stop. Even if kissing him was a mistake.

He kissed her back, harder than before. His other arm crept around her. She shivered when his hand touched the bare skin of her back.

She barely ran her hand through his hair when he pulled back again.

She opened her eyes. "What are you doing?" Reality struck her. She really just kissed him. Or he kissed her.

He met her gaze but remained silent. His mouth moved slightly, like he was going to say something but couldn't remember how to talk.

She pulled her hand from his chest and stepped back. "I

really should finish getting ready. My hair and makeup . . ." She touched her hand to her head.

He cleared his throat. "Sorry, I just thought you . . ." He turned around and walked toward his suitcase and started rummaging through it. "I figured it would be better to practice kissing in the hotel room."

"What?" She spoke louder than she meant.

"That's part of our agreement, right? You wanted to kiss a few times at the wedding reception? Since we are dating."

She nodded slowly, even though he couldn't see because he was still rummaging in his suitcase. He waited another moment before pulling out a small comb and standing up.

His voice was still husky when he spoke. "I just thought we should practice so we don't have an awkward kiss at the reception. You know, in case it's awkward to kiss each other." He stopped talking abruptly and walked out of the room to the outer room of the suite. He closed the door behind him, leaving her alone.

She let out a huff of air. Did that really just happen? Had Bill gotten more flustered by their kiss than her?

She walked to the mirror and studied her reflection.

She really liked this dress.

BILL

Bill silently held open the passenger door for Emily. She brushed past him, leaving a whisper of perfume in her path. He inhaled deeply as she settled herself into the car seat.

She looked amazing. After his embarrassing attempt at a kiss, she did something to her hair so that it had loose curls tied back in some type of low ponytail or bun or whatever women called it when their hair was gathered in the back. He should know what that was called. He had dated other women, after all.

But none like Emily.

Her makeup looked amazing too. She took his breath away.

He climbed into the driver seat and slowly pulled the car out of the parking lot. He remembered, too late, that he didn't know where they were going.

"Which way?" He stopped the car at the exit of the parking lot and glanced at her.

She didn't even look at the address on the invitation. "Left, then take the second right. That will put you on the main road. The church is a few miles down that street. It will be impossible to miss." She bit her bottom lip lightly, the same way she did after they finished kissing. Her cheeks flushed lightly, almost as if she were also thinking of their kiss. But was she? She barely reacted to his kiss earlier. And he wasn't a bad kisser. At least, he didn't think he was a bad kisser.

He pressed the gas pedal to drive. They both lurched forward as the car jolted into action.

He gritted his teeth. Since when did he forget how to drive?

He focused on getting to the main road before attempting to talk to her again. "Your hair looks nice." He took his eyes off the road long enough to see her give him a sideways glance. "Your bun is good." He cringed as the words came out.

She let out a quiet hum. "Thanks. It's actually a simple version of a ponytail. My friend Theresa showed me how to do it the other day."

"Theresa . . . is that the same woman who was in the car with you when I called? The one who asked about your boobs?" He cringed again. What was wrong with his brain? One little kiss, a kiss that didn't even last that long, turned him into a babbling fool. "You know, when you were talking about dress shopping? That's what I meant to say. I didn't mean to talk about your body." He took a deep breath in and tried again. "Your hair looks very pretty."

"Thanks. And yes, that was Theresa." She let out a small laugh. "She's new at work, so I've been helping her out. She's pretty nice. She even video chatted with me earlier so she could help me with my makeup. I don't usually wear this much makeup." She pulled down the visor and flipped open the small mirror to inspect her face as she spoke. "Anyway, I thought that I could set you two up after we get back. You know, as a thank-you for your help this weekend."

He focused on keeping the car on the road. She really shouldn't say things like that when he was driving. She obviously had no idea what type of impact she had on him.

He needed to choose his words carefully. The only person he wanted to date right now was Emily. And he could only date her if he didn't move back to his hometown. But he had to move back.

He really didn't want to think about that anymore today.

He couldn't lie, though. "I'm actually taking a break from dating."

"What?" Her voice was oddly loud.

He tried to glance at her without her noticing. "I'm pretty busy these days and haven't gone on a date for a few months. This weekend is the one exception."

"What about Meredith?"

He looked at her automatically, just in time to see her clasp her hand over her mouth. He didn't care that she saw his phone, but her reaction surprised him. "Mere—"

She interrupted. "Don't answer that. It's none of my business. I really didn't mean to look at your phone earlier. I heard the text and thought it was my phone. I didn't realize my mistake until after I already read the text. Please forget that I said anything."

He held back a smile. She couldn't be jealous, could she? She'd been sending him signal after signal that she didn't think of him as someone she would date, but that kiss had suggested otherwise. And now this.

"Fine," he said. "But if you change your mind—"

"Nope. Not interested in knowing. I am not going to pry into your personal life."

"Fine." He fought the temptation to tell her anyway, just to see the look on her face when she found out that Meredith was married to his best friend from high school. Meredith had enthusiastically organized a small family dinner to celebrate his upcoming move back to their town.

Would she look relieved to know that Meredith wasn't a girlfriend? Or would she not care?

"How much farther to the church?"

"Just a little farther up this road."

As he drove around a bend in the road, a small tree limb appeared up ahead. He swerved harder than necessary to avoid it, then checked his rearview mirror automatically before stealing a glance at Emily.

Something like that wouldn't normally bother him while driving. His PTSD symptoms must be worse because of the run-in with Ethan. He'd been on edge walking through the lobby, felt a never-ending tightness in his chest, and had his first nightmare in months last night. Plus, he nearly jumped out of his skin when he thought he saw someone in the lobby who'd lost his arm overseas. His heart didn't stop racing for several minutes after he realized his mistake. He scratched his neck, then replaced his hand on the steering wheel.

He needed to be careful and regain control of himself and his PTSD. Emily's mere presence jumbled his brain and made it hard to focus on anything except her. They only had this weekend together. He did not want her to start thinking of him as a broken man, stuck in the past and scared of his own shadow.

Anyone who'd been through what he'd experienced would have similar scars. He didn't always believe that, but he had eventually realized the truth. Scars could be visible or invisible. He didn't want to explain that to Emily.

He wanted her to see the best in him. Not the worst.

He wanted to just have one last weekend of freedom before giving up the job he loved, the city he loved, and the life he loved in order to help take care of his parents.

No, what he really wanted was a chance with Emily.

He squeezed the steering wheel tightly.

Fortunately, Emily spoke again before the silence grew too awkward. "There's the church. The parking lot entrance is on the right."

He pulled into the parking lot and, minutes later, escorted Emily down the paved sidewalk towards the church entrance, her hand securely in his. Someone had spent a lot of time and effort putting flowers and decorations throughout the entryway and among the seats, and an usher stood at the door, dressed in a tuxedo with a forest green tie.

Emily tensed at his side. "That's Sam. I can't do this."

"Want to turn back?" Bill eyed the front of the church.

"No."

"We can sit in the back. I actually prefer the back of large rooms." He tried to look normal as he spoke, like he wasn't admitting that he was as nervous as she was about the wedding, but for different reasons.

"Why do you like the back of the room?" Emily spoke quietly as they approached the steps.

Bill squeezed her hand. Easier to keep an eye on who enters and leaves the room, easier to protect yourself if something bad happened, less risk of a surprise attack. But he wasn't going to say that. "No one will care if you skip the ceremony and go to the reception."

She bit her lip and shook her head. "I'm already here. Sam saw us. I can't turn back now."

"Sam?"

She gripped Bill's hand tighter and started up the steep stone steps. "I'll handle this." Her voice contained an edge that he hadn't heard before.

"You didn't include a guest on the RSVP." The usher at the door curled his lips into a sneer as they reached the top step.

Bill straightened his back and widened his stance slightly. There was something about the way Sam looked at Emily that unsettled him. He agreed to let Emily handle this situation, but he might change his mind. Sam had an athletic build, like someone who spent hours at the gym lifting weights. If it came down to a fight, it would be a close call.

"Hello Sam." Emily's voice was guarded.

Sam stared at Bill but spoke to Emily. "We were taking bets on whether you'd show up."

"We can seat ourselves." Emily tugged on Bill's hand to move, but Sam still blocked the doorway.

"Guess I owe ten dollars to a few of the guys."

Bill gritted his teeth but let Emily take the lead. She looked at Sam for a second, then tried to walk around him again.

"Wait" Sam shifted slightly, relaxing his shoulders and speaking in a quieter voice, like he realized he needed to change tactics if he wanted to talk with Emily. He stepped closer to Emily.

Bill instinctively released Emily's hand and wrapped his arm around her shoulder, pulling her close to his side.

"It doesn't have to be like this." Sam lowered his voice but still sounded like a snake in the weeds. He cleared his throat and addressed Bill. "Give us a minute alone."

Emily spoke before Bill could respond. "I don't want a minute alone with you, Sam. I've told you that before."

"You think bringing a guy like this would stop me?"

"That's not why I brought him."

"Then stop playing games and ignoring me." His voice was laced with anger, making Bill tense.

"There's nothing between us, Sam."

"You think this guy is better than me?"

"She said she doesn't want to talk with you. Leave her alone. Move." Bill didn't need to hear another word from Sam. It was obvious by his tone and the way he looked at Emily that something had happened between them. She didn't mention dating anyone since Ethan, but maybe she'd turned him down for a date? But why didn't she mention that? And did this guy really think that he had a chance of stealing Emily away from him? Bill eyed him carefully, memorizing everything about his appearance. This man wouldn't get the chance to be anywhere near Emily for the rest of the day.

"Emily, you know that you want to talk with me. You know this isn't over."

Bill glanced at Emily, who looked at him with wide eyes. All the color had drained from her face. She moved her head so slightly that he wasn't sure if he imagined it.

Didn't matter. Bill tightened his grip around Emily's side, pushing her slightly behind him. "No."

"We have personal things to discuss."

"Not with my girlfriend."

"Emily can make her own choices." Sam pushed out his chest and crossed his arms.

"She made her choice. She's here with me. You want to talk with her, you talk with me too."

"Sam, there's nothing to talk about." Emily spoke, but Sam didn't look at her.

"You going to hold on to her all day?"

"I'll hold her as long as she lets me. Only a fool would let her go."

Sam's face reddened.

Emily pressed her body against Bill's. "Let's go inside."

Sam didn't move out of their path, so Bill took a step closer and raised his chin. "She said she wants to go inside."

Sam narrowed his eyes. "How much did you pay for your bodyguard, Emily?"

"Step aside, Sam." Bill tried to hold back the growl in his voice. "I'm warning you."

"Emily, all I want is five minutes."

"We don't care what you want." Bill sucked in a deep breath. "Final warning, Sam."

Sam uncrossed his arms like he was preparing to fight. Bill removed his arm from around Emily.

Another tuxedo-clad man stepped out on the entrance of the church. This guy looked thinner and a few years older than Sam. Flecks of grey marked his dark hair. "Men, everything ok out here? Emily?" No one spoke for a few seconds. "Wedding is about to start. Time to head inside."

Sam relaxed his stance slightly, and Bill stepped back and wrapped his arm around Emily again.

Emily looked at the new arrival. "We'll find our own seats."

He looked at Bill and Sam. "Sam, you're needed at the altar."

Sam crossed his arms again and stared at Emily. "I'll find you at the reception."

Bill moved his arm to release Emily, but the new man stepped between them. "Sam, altar, now."

Sam gave Emily one last look before he turned and walked away.

Bill opened his mouth to speak to Emily, but the new man cleared his throat.

"All guests inside, please. Follow me." His voice was heavy with caution but no immediate threat.

Bill waited to see if Emily would follow. If she showed any sign of hesitation, he'd pick her up and run to the parking lot. Get her away from Sam and whatever it was he wanted.

But Emily moved out from under his arm and stepped forward through the doorway into the church.

22

BILL

The church was as bad as he thought it would be: rows upon rows of seats, with stained glass windows on three of the four walls. Doors were leading in and out of the sanctuary in the front, left, and back walls. No matter where they sat, he wouldn't be able to keep an eye on each of the entry points to the room. Not to mention that the room was already close to being full. There must have been over a hundred guests.

The familiar beads of sweat started to break out over his forehead. One of the many tortures of his version of PTSD was never to feel comfortable in a crowded room. Monitoring all entry points only took the edge off the fear.

He thought he'd be able to manage a room like this today. But seeing Ethan brought forward too many bad memories of deployment. And whatever happened outside with Sam made him even more hypervigilant.

He glanced at Emily. She had a smile on her face and was waving to someone farther ahead. She tugged on his hand, and he followed. He needed to think of a plan. If he could manage sitting in the room until the ceremony started, maybe he could sneak away without anyone's notice.

Emily led him halfway up the rows and stopped in front of someone. Her mom.

Cheryl stood up and gave Emily a hug. Bill tried his best to act normally when she turned and hugged him. "I saved you both some seats." She motioned at two seats farther down the aisle. "Your father is around here, somewhere, Emily. He's excited to meet Bill." She gave Emily a small nudge.

Bill scratched his neck uncomfortably. Just looking at the seats, in the middle of the row, with people sitting in front, in back, and on both sides, made him feel sick.

He cleared his throat and looked at Emily. She and her mother were deep in conversation already. He had a few seconds to decide whether to act like a controlling jerk and drag her to a different pair of seats, or endure the torture of sitting in the seats her mother chose.

Who was he kidding? He wouldn't last more than five minutes in the seats her mother chose.

This whole plan was a mistake. He should never have agreed to come with Emily. And he definitely should never have pretended that someone like him could be with someone as perfect as her.

He needed to escape.

Emily took a step back from her mother and looked expectantly at him. He swallowed uncomfortably. She and her mother both expected a response from him, but he hadn't heard the question.

"Bill? Everything ok?" Emily asked curiously.

He nodded and tried his best to look relaxed, then scanned the room behind her.

When he looked at her again, her expression had changed. She no longer looked curious but had that stubborn look that meant she was about to put up a fight.

His breath caught in his throat. He needed to stay calm.

He looked over at Emily's mother. "Cheryl, it's nice to see you, but—"

"Mom," Emily interrupted Bill and gave him a pointed look. "Thanks for saving the seats for us. However, Bill and I would be more comfortable closer to the back."

Cheryl's brow wrinkled. "I got here early to save the seats, just like you asked. In the middle, not too close to the front, but close enough that it was clear that you weren't hiding from anyone. Are you ok? Did you change your mind?" She lowered her voice to a whisper, but even her whisper was loud enough for Bill to hear. "I thought you wanted to make sure that no one thought you were hiding or heartbroken."

Bill watched Emily's face closely. If he were a better man, he'd be able to sit where Emily was most comfortable. He clenched his jaw. He could handle sitting there for half an hour. The ceremony couldn't possibly be longer than that. He'd done harder things in his life. He could sit and pretend that he was comfortable without giving in to the urge to run away to somewhere safe.

Emily shook her head. "The seats are perfect, Mom. I just changed my mind."

Cheryl gave Emily one last concerned look. "Alright. I'll see you at the reception."

Emily tugged his hand again and directed him to the back of the room.

"What was that about, Emily? You ok?" He carefully controlled his voice as he spoke, trying not to let her hear any signs of panic.

"I don't feel like sitting so close to the front. No one will notice us in the back."

She walked to the last row of seats and turned, leading him along the back wall until they reached the corner. She pointed to the last two seats in the row. "These seats ok?"

He glanced around. A few people smiled in greeting as

she sat down carefully in her seat. The church was almost full, but at least no one could sit behind them. The seat Emily picked out also afforded him a view of all entrances into the room.

He sighed a breath of relief. He could manage to get through the ceremony from this position in the church.

He sat down next to her and wiped his brow. She looked around the room.

"Thanks for helping me with the Sam situation. I'm really glad you came here with me."

Her smile cast some type of spell over him, and he felt his anxiety lessen while something else crept in. "Me too. Sam is a jerk."

She let out a small laugh. "He really is." She bit her lip, then looked at Bill hesitantly.

He reached for her hand and held it gently. "I won't let anyone treat you poorly."

She squeezed his hand. "Thanks. I think the worst is over, though. I just didn't expect to see Sam right away. He and Ethan were friends since high school. We hung out together a lot of times, but I never trusted Sam. Anyway, after Ethan and I broke up, Sam asked me out. Many times. I kept saying no, and he wasn't happy about that. I had to block his phone number."

Bill's stomach turned into knots. "Do I need to talk to him at the reception?"

"No. I think he already got the message."

Bill placed his hand on her cheek. "I'll do whatever you need me to do to protect you."

She shivered slightly under his light touch. He liked that.

"Do you ever need protecting?" she asked, looking deep into his eyes.

He tried to break eye contact but couldn't. It was like she could read him like a book, figure out all his secrets if she kept staring into his eyes like that. He felt exposed. Vulnerable.

Her eyes lowered to his lips. "Now would be a good time to kiss me. Just a quick one. To send a clear message."

"What message is that?"

"That I'm your girlfriend."

He leaned in closer. "That would send a clear message."

"Is that a yes?" She barely managed to speak.

He leaned forward. His lips barely grazed across hers when music started playing. He jumped, startled by the noise.

The wedding had started. By the time he looked back at Emily, her back was to him, watching the bridal party as they began their walk down the aisle.

23

EMILY

The ceremony had ended an hour ago. Emily watched Veronica walk down the aisle in her white wedding dress to meet the man Emily had planned on marrying up until a few short months ago. She listened to Veronica vow to remain faithful to the man who broke her own heart. She sat calmly as Veronica kissed the man Emily had kissed countless times over the past two years. She even clapped as the bride and groom walked out of the church together.

Enough time passed since the ceremony ended for her and Bill to drive to the boat dock and climb aboard the ship for the cruise around the lake.

Enough time passed since the ceremony that she should have felt something by now. Any emotion. Sadness, heart-break, devastation, rejection. But she felt nothing except relief.

She stepped through the door to an elegantly decorated ballroom on the ship. Large glass windows lined the wall, giving breath-taking views of the surrounding lake and mountains. A tall wedding cake adorned with intricately woven icing stood in one corner of the room, while a small band played music by the dance floor at the other end of the room. Scattered throughout the room were tables with white tablecloths, each marked with a number.

She scanned the room for table six, where she and Bill were assigned to sit. Bill stood silently next to her. She located the table first, in the middle of the room but hesitated and glanced at Bill.

"Our table is over there." She pointed in the general direction of their table, watching him closely. His eyes narrowed. She could almost hear the thoughts running through his head.

Just as she anticipated, he did that funny thing with his face where he tensed his jaw and puffed his chest, like he was preparing to face something unpleasant.

That settled the matter in her mind. "I know it's bad manners, but I see some people I know at table ten. I'm going to see if I can switch our seats. I'll be right back. Can you get me something to drink?"

She left Bill on his own and walked up to an elderly couple who were already seated at the table in the corner. They looked up at her expectantly. She put on a large smile. "Excuse me, but could you please switch seats with my boyfriend and I? We are supposed to be at table six, up front, but I get motion sickness and would feel much better if I was near the back of the room in case I need to make a quick exit."

The couple looked at each other. Emily tried not to think too hard about the lie she just told. It wasn't really a lie, anyway. As much as she hoped that the medicated patch from Bill would work, she still had her doubts.

The elderly lady leaned over and spoke to the man who Emily assumed was her husband. "That's the woman."

The old man stuck his finger in his ear and adjusted

something. He pulled his hand away and Emily saw a hearing aid. "What?" His voice was loud.

"That's the woman, Bert." The old lady spoke louder in the direction of his ear and pointed at Emily. "Ethan warned me about her."

"What woman?"

"The one Ethan dumped. The crazy one. She crashed his car." The elderly woman spoke directly in his ear, loud enough for anyone to hear.

Emily fought the urge to roll her eyes. They must be Ethan's relatives. "I didn't crash his car. It was a minor fender bender, months before we broke up, and I paid for the repairs."

"What'd she say?" Bert looked at his wife.

"She said she didn't crash his car."

"Who cares? What time is the food coming out?" Bert adjusted his hearing aid again.

"Don't know. You want a snack?" She started rummaging in her purse.

Emily shuffled uncomfortably before speaking again, louder than before. "Do you mind changing seats with my boyfriend and me? I get motion sickness and want to be close to the exit. Our seats are closer to the bridal party and the dance floor."

The woman didn't even look up from her purse. "I don't dance." She pulled a peppermint candy out from the depths of her bag and held it up to Bert. "Here."

He glanced at it. "That's a mint. I want food."

"I don't have any. That's what you get." She started looking through her purse again.

Bert looked from his wife to Emily as if he just noticed her standing next to them. "What do you want?"

"I just wanted to ask if—"

"There's food over there. Go get me a plate." Bert pointed

while yelling.

Emily glanced over her shoulder at the area where the caterers were setting up the buffet. "I don't think they are ready to start serving yet."

His wife let out a loud snort. "Hmph. Since when do you care about other people's feelings?"

Emily's jaw dropped open. "I didn't mean to upset you. I just came over here to ask—"

"Ruth, what's she doing? And where's my food?" Bert put his finger to his ear again, as if that would make his hearing aid work better.

Emily let out an exasperated sigh and stalked over to the caterer's table. She caught the attention of one of the servers. "Excuse me, do you have some bread or something small for him to eat?" She pointed to the couple she just left.

The server nodded and motioned to a small basket at the end of the table. "There are some rolls at the end of the table. Help yourself."

Emily grabbed a small roll, placed it on a plate, and walked back to the table.

The old couple looked up at her like she was an alien.

Ruth frowned while Bert leaned over to her and spoke. "Why'd she come back? Think she's trying to steal something? Hold your purse tight."

"She's not going to steal anything from me, not if I can help it. Ethan was right to dump her. Said she lied too much. And couldn't cook."

Emily stopped next to them and gathered her courage. She hadn't fit the puzzle pieces together until hours after Ethan mentioned that they were both in the military. Some military guys came back with invisible scars, like post-traumatic stress disorder.

Now that she suspected PTSD, she couldn't make Bill sit in the middle of the ballroom, surrounded by strangers on all sides. She tried to remember everything she'd learned about PTSD during college. Hypervigilance, anxiety in large crowds, trouble feeling safe. If he had PTSD, all of Bill's actions made sense. His insistence on sitting next to the wall at the restaurant, switching tables at the coffee shop, driving in order not to give up control of the car, and the thorough search of their hotel room last night. Even the expression on his face when they entered the church.

She glanced across the room at Bill, who waited in line for a drink at the cash bar. She made up her mind.

The old couple was still staring at her.

"Here's a dinner roll. One of the caterers said you could have it." She held out the offering to Bert, who eyed her suspiciously.

"What's that for?" His voice was even louder than before.

"You said you were hungry." She set the plate down in front of him.

"Bert, don't eat that." Ruth grabbed the plate and pushed it aside surprisingly fast. "She stole that food."

"Ethan said she's a thief. Stole his car once." Bert poked his hearing aid again with his finger.

"No, she crashed his car." Ruth corrected him. "She stole all the pots and pans from his kitchen."

Emily's face started to burn. She glanced again at Bill, who still stood in line for a drink. "I didn't steal anything from him, and it was a minor car accident. I paid for all the repairs."

They both stared at her like she had two heads. Bert turned back to Ruth. "Why'd she steal all the kitchen things if she can't cook?"

"She probably sold them for drug money or something. Can't trust a woman like that. Ethan's lucky he got away," Ruth said.

Emily took a deep breath in. "Would you like to switch

tables with me? My boyfriend and I have seats near the front, close to the buffet line. You'll also be closer to the bride and groom's table." She crossed her fingers behind her back.

Bert picked up the bread roll and sniffed it. "Do you think she did something to this bread?"

Ruth leaned over to smell it too. "Don't eat it. She's trying to bribe you. She wants our seats."

"Why does she want our seats?" Bert looked up at Emily.

Finally, maybe they were getting somewhere. "I get motion sickness, and your table is closer to the bathroom."

Ruth leaned over and whispered in Bert's ear, loud enough for anyone standing within ten feet to hear. "She said she's sick. Don't touch that food. It's contaminated." Ruth started rummaging through her purse.

Bert stabbed the dinner roll with a fork and held it up for inspection. "Looks normal to me." He sniffed it again.

"I'm not sick. But I get motion sick on boats and want to sit closer to the bathroom," Emily explained.

Bert kept examining the bread roll. "The bathroom is around the corner."

"Yes, I know. I—"

"Here, Bert." Ruth snatched the fork and roll from Bert's hand and put it on the plate before drowning his hands with hand sanitizer. "Rub your hands together."

"I know what to do." He scowled and wiped his hands on a cloth napkin.

Emily groaned, recognizing her failure. "Sorry, I didn't mean to bother you. Hope you have a nice time today."

"Wait just a minute." Ruth pointed her finger at Emily. "I heard all about what you did to Ethan. Don't start thinking that you can win him back through us. We aren't going to fall for your tricks. He just got married. He doesn't want you."

Emily tried not to flinch. "I'm actually here with a date.

And I'm very happy for the bride and groom." Or at least she was happy that she hadn't married Ethan.

Ruth sneered and nudged Bert. "She said she's here with a date. I told you she's a liar."

Emily scanned the room but didn't see Bill. "I—"

"Where's the butter?" Bert looked at her accusingly.

"Butter?" Emily asked.

"For the bread." He held up the fork with the roll still attached. "Who gets someone bread without butter?"

Emily counted to three. "It was good meeting you both. I'll —"

"Ethan always said she was selfish. Even crashed his car because it was nicer than hers." Ruth scowled at Emily.

She gritted her teeth. "I did not crash his car. I mean, I did, but it was an accident."

"I never crashed a car." Ruth looked like she was about to say more but stopped the moment an arm wrapped around Emily's shoulder. She leaned over to Bert again. "Look at that, she's letting this guy put his arm around her. Women these days have no morals. Ethan just dumped her, and she's already hooking up with someone else. That's what kids call it these days. Hooking up."

Emily resisted scowling back at Ruth and looked at Bill. He raised his eyebrows and turned to Ruth and Bert. "Mind if I steal her?"

Bert adjusted his hearing aid again. "She stole this bread, not me."

A muscle twitched in Bill's jaw. "I'll make sure she doesn't steal anything else."

Emily kicked him subtly. "Don't encourage—"

"Where's my butter?" Bert yelled louder than necessary.

Emily sighed and looked at Bill. "Let's get out of here."

She turned around and started walking to their assigned table. There was obviously no point in trying to change seats with that couple, or anyone at their table, unless she wanted to spend the entire reception listening to their criticisms. She made it halfway to the table before her guilt took over. She stopped, walked to the buffet stand, and grabbed two small packets of butter.

She walked back to Bert and Ruth, who had been joined by three other elderly people.

"Here." She set the butter on the table next to Bert and turned to walk away.

"What was that about? Don't touch that butter, Bert. She probably stole it." Ruth's voice carried until she got farther away.

Emily stalked to the front of the room and tried not to collapse into her seat at table six. What had Ethan told people about her? Even that old couple, who Emily didn't recognize despite dating Ethan for years and meeting most of his family, recognized her as Ethan's ex-girlfriend.

She scanned the room, trying not to make eye contact with anyone. Only one other table stood in a corner, but it was farthest from the exit. That table might be more comfortable for Bill—if he even had PTSD. Maybe he didn't. She was only guessing. Was it really worth going to another table to ask about switching seats if she didn't actually know if he had PTSD?

Anyway, if they did sit at that other corner table, she'd have to run across the entire room to reach the exit if she got sick.

She crossed her arms and leaned back in her seat. They were stuck at table six, in the front and center of the room, with nowhere to hide from prying eyes.

At least she had Bill with her. Any guests who wanted to pity or judge her for losing Ethan would see that she had clearly moved on.

But where was Bill?

She scanned the room again, this time looking for her date. He looked engrossed in a conversation with a woman she didn't recognize. She looked younger, maybe in her mid-twenties, and gorgeous. Emily narrowed her eyes as this woman laughed at something Bill said and placed her hand on his shoulder.

This reception was turning into a nightmare, and the boat hadn't even left the dock yet.

24

EMILY

She needed something to do before anyone noticed her sitting alone while her fake boyfriend collected phone numbers from gorgeous women. She pulled her phone out of her purse and focused on the screen. She opened her texts. No new texts.

Her eyes moved upwards on their own. At least that woman had removed her hand from Bill's shoulder.

She opened her email. One new email from Theresa showed up.

Emily's stomach flipped. When they were video chatting earlier, Theresa said she'd start a dating profile for her, but she didn't think she'd start it that quickly.

She opened the email and scanned the message from Theresa. She had included a username and password along with a link. She clicked the link and downloaded the dating app.

She glanced up quickly. Another woman had joined Bill, so now, two gorgeous women fought for his attention.

She looked back at the phone and opened the newly

downloaded app. She bit her lip. If she really wanted to get back out in the dating world, she needed to do this.

Emily squeezed her eyes shut. All she had to do was type in a few letters and numbers. Theresa already did the hard part. She gave Theresa permission to write up a profile for her and post her pic. All she had to do at this point was log in and start looking through the eligible guys.

Someone pulled out the chair next to her. She opened her eyes and clutched her phone.

Bill let out a quiet groan as he sat next to her. "I helped you get away from that old couple. Why didn't you rescue me from those women?"

Emily checked her phone to make sure the screen was off. "I thought we had an agreement. You don't flirt with other women during the reception."

"If you walked over, you would know that I wasn't flirting."

Emily shrugged. He slid a glass of wine in front of her. "Where'd that come from?"

"I got it while you were busy making friends with that old couple."

"Hmph." She took a sip.

"Usually, girlfriends say thank you when their boyfriends get them a glass of wine." His voice was light and teasing.

"Usually, boyfriends get in trouble for openly flirting with other women." She took another sip. She tipped the glass and studied the color of the liquid inside, which was suspiciously pale.

"Something wrong with your drink?" He whispered into her ear.

She tried not to shiver. Why did he always have to whisper in her ear? Did he know the effect that had on her?

"What kind of wine is this?" she asked.

He shrugged and took a sip of his own drink.

"Did you get me a glass of grape juice?"

He didn't respond right away, but the twitching muscle in his jaw betrayed his silence.

"You did, didn't you? Why would you get me grape juice instead of wine? Is this your idea of a joke?" She reached for his glass.

He moved faster than her and slid his glass away. He leaned in close again. She stiffened. She was not going to let him know how much it affected her when he was that close.

He started whispering, loud enough that only she could hear. "You can't drink wine since you have that motion sickness patch." He ran his hand along her hair, tracing the outline of the patch he placed on her earlier that day. "I didn't want anyone to make bad guesses about why you aren't drinking, so I got you a glass of non-alcoholic white wine. White grape juice. Your welcome."

She turned her head. He really did think of every detail. She opened her mouth to speak when her parents approached. Emily turned to them instead, offering them a forced smile while they seated themselves across from her and Bill. "Hi Mom, Dad."

"Emily, Bill, good to see you both." Her mother offered a warm smile while Bill rose to shake hands with her father.

Emily chatted with her parents for a few minutes, who sat down in their assigned seats at the table. At least she didn't have to worry about Bill flirting with anyone at their table. She checked the other place settings and saw some other, older relatives of hers were assigned to the remaining empty seats. No one under the age of fifty was going to join them.

As they talked, Emily stole glances at Bill. He looked a little tense, scanning the room occasionally, but it appeared he enjoyed the conversation with her parents.

She frowned. That conversation with the old couple had been a waste of time. Actually, this whole weekend was a waste of time. Did she really think that Bill would be interested in her when there was a room full of bridesmaids and other single women who were all thinking about falling in love and having a wedding of their own? She could be home right now, watching a movie or taking a nap or swiping left and right on the dating app.

Bill chose that minute to lean over and whisper. "Is now a good time to kiss you?"

Emily tried to look unaffected. "Why would you do that?"

"Look to your right."

Emily couldn't help herself. She looked and cringed. The first flirty woman didn't stop staring at Bill even when Emily looked. She just smiled, raised her glass of wine, and took a slow sip.

Emily turned back to Bill. "Is she your type?" She was gorgeous. No one could doubt that.

Bill wrapped his arm around her. "You really should kiss me now if you want Clare to back off."

"My parents are here."

"They aren't paying attention."

Emily glanced up. He was right. They, along with almost every other wedding guest, were looking at the dance floor as the bridal party made their entrance.

She glanced over at Clare. She definitely was not watching the bridal party.

"Fine. Let's kiss." She leaned forward expectantly.

Bill moved his head back but kept his arm around her. "Not so fast. I only kiss willing participants."

"What are you talking about? I'm willing." She tried to move forward again, but he pulled back farther.

"Let me rephrase that. I'm not that good of an actor. If we kiss, it needs to be real. Not just a quick kiss to convince anyone that this is real."

"You are a tease. You started this conversation and asked for the kiss," Emily said, trying to sound irritated but failing.

He winked and stood up, pulling her up with him. All the other guests were already standing and cheering as the bride and groom walked in.

Emily sighed. "At least we can get our food soon. I'm starving."

"Should have stolen an extra roll and butter for yourself."

"I didn't steal anything."

"Are you going to tell me that you didn't also crash Ethan's car?" He politely clapped while talking.

She elbowed him. "I didn't crash it. It was a minor fender bender, and I wasn't even at fault. I paid for the repairs."

He shrugged like he didn't believe her, but his face looked amused.

She elbowed him again. "It's true! Someone rear-ended me at a traffic light, just messed up the back bumper." She couldn't help feeling a jolt from the teasing look on his face. Like she was the only person in the room who mattered to him. Like she was the only person he wanted to talk with.

He reached for her hand and sat down as all the other guests also sat. Emily glanced around the room. Clare still stared at Bill.

He leaned over to her again. "Why were you even over there, talking with that couple?"

Emily inhaled deeply and tried to focus. Her brain was threatening to stop working. "I wanted to switch tables."

"Why?"

"You'll laugh if I tell you." She had been so sure that he had PTSD when she walked over to that table, but she must have been wrong. He seemed to have no trouble sitting at this table in the center of the room.

"I promise I won't." He held up his hand, pinky towards her. "I pinky promise."

"Pinky promise? I haven't made a pinky promise since I was eight."

"Maybe you should try it again." He picked up her hand and latched his pinky around hers. "There. Done."

She hesitated. There really wasn't any harm in telling him the truth. Other than feeling massive amounts of embarrassment. "I'll answer your question if you answer my questions." She lifted her glass of grape juice to her lips. Even if it wasn't wine, she needed something to drink. Her mouth had gone dry.

A crooked grin formed on his face. "Let's make this more interesting. Truth or dare?"

She tried not to snort on her juice. "Are you serious?"

"Dead serious." He crossed his arms. "Or we can just sit here and make polite, boring conversation."

"Fine. My turn first. Why do you travel with a fish named Boo Boo?" Emily thought of the small fish who'd been swimming laps in the glass jar on the counter of their hotel suite all morning.

"His name is Boo Boo the Second, and he was a gift for someone. My nephew."

Emily raised her eyebrows in surprise. "Does your family live near here? Is that where you went this morning?"

He held up his hand to stop her. "You asked your question already. It's my turn."

She shrugged reluctantly. "Fine. I went by that table to see if they would switch seats with us. You know, because I get motion sickness and that table is closer to the exit." She looked out the window. The boat had started moving at some point, and she didn't feel any signs of motion sickness.

He narrowed his eyes. "The game is called truth or dare. Tell the truth."

"How could you tell that wasn't the truth?"

"You scratch your ear when you are trying to hide something."

She lowered her hand from her ear.

"So, what's the real reason you wanted to switch tables? I know it's not because of motion sickness, because that patch should work."

She let out a deep breath. "Fine. I was trying to figure you out. I thought you had PTSD." She watched his eyes but his face remained blank. Maybe he didn't know what PTSD meant. "Ethan said you guys deployed at the same time while you were both in the military. I don't know what you saw or did there, but I know that some people come back from deployment with memories that still haunt them. You refused to let me drive. You searched the hotel room when we got there. Plus, each time we've met at a restaurant, you scan the room. At first, I thought you were just looking for women to hit on. But then I realized it might be something different."

No emotion showed on his face.

Emily worried that she made a mistake. "I didn't want to say anything in case I was wrong."

Out of the corner of her eye, she saw everyone at her table rise and walk towards the buffet table. Emily and Bill sat alone.

Bill's face could have been made out of stone. She waited, wondering how much time would pass before he responded.

Finally, he silently took her hand, stood up, and led her to join the other guests at the buffet line.

25

BILL

Bill glanced around the room again. He couldn't help himself. It was a reflexive action, as automatic as breathing or blinking.

The plates had been cleared away, and the dance floor was slowly filling with guests. Bill tried to loosen his tie slightly. The room was stifling but bearable.

He reached for Emily's hand. Like each other time, she inhaled sharply when they touched. He didn't think she realized that she had that reaction. But he liked it.

Now that the shock over her suspicion that he had PTSD passed, all he wanted was time alone with her. To talk. To get to know everything about her. Understand how she was able to figure out something that some of his closest friends hadn't known. And find out why she wanted to stick by his side instead of abandoning him in search of someone who didn't feel broken inside.

He leaned forward to whisper in her ear, watching her face. He wasn't disappointed. She bit her lip as soon as his mouth got close to her ear.

"Want to go out on the deck? Get some fresh air?" He let

his lip brush her ear. He knew better than to play with her reactions, but he couldn't resist seeing her shiver, bite her lip, or blush each time he got close.

She swallowed and nodded without turning her head towards him.

He started to stand but stopped as the band stopped playing a song and the lead singer's voice rang out over the crowd.

"Single ladies, get ready! One more song and then it's time for the bouquet toss!"

A loud cheer rang from one of the nearby tables as a large group of women made their way to the front of the room to dance until it was time to catch the flowers and dream about being the next woman in the crowd to stand at the altar.

Bill glanced at Emily. She sat motionless in the chair.

"I'm not going up there." She managed to speak without moving her mouth.

"Fine with me." He wrapped his arm around her shoulder.

"I'm not ashamed to be single. It's nothing like that. I'd like to get married one day. But I'm not going up there."

"That's fine."

"I just don't feel like standing up there, waiting to catch the bouquet."

"No one expects you to go up there."

"I don't know why anyone thinks the bouquet toss is a good idea."

"I thought women liked it?"

Emily looked at him like he had two heads. "There's no way I'm going to walk to the front of the room and announce to everyone here that I'm single, especially when I was supposed to marry the groom. It'd be humiliating."

"We can tell everyone that we're engaged." He didn't know where the words came from, but they shocked him as much as they shocked Emily. But part of him hoped she'd agree.

She recovered quickly. "I don't have a ring. No one would believe the lie."

"We'll say the ring is getting resized."

"They'll ask what the ring looks like."

He held back a smirk and picked up her left hand, running a finger lightly over her ring finger. "Diamonds are traditional, but I'd give you something unique. Maybe an emerald."

She shook her head. "I don't like green."

"Aquamarine?"

She narrowed her eyes like she was imagining a pale blue gemstone on her hand. "Maybe."

He pulled her hand closer to his chest, still focused on her fingers. "Sapphire."

She shuddered. "Ethan gave me his grandmother's ring. It had sapphire stones around the diamond."

"No sapphire." He focused as he tried to pick the right stone for her. Her dress was a deep shade of purple, and complimented her skin perfectly. But would she want an amethyst ring to match the dress? He lifted her hand to his mouth and placed a gentle kiss on the spot where an engagement ring belonged and had a flash of inspiration. "Opal."

"Opal?" Her voice sounded strained, like she was trying to catch her breath.

He kissed the spot on her hand one more time as he made up his mind. "Opals have a pearly white color, with different sheens of color throughout. It shines differently when you move it in the sunlight. Different angles bring out different images. There's something deep and captivating about them."

"Sounds perfect."

Something stirred inside Bill. He shifted slightly and reached for her chin. She looked at him, just as he hoped she would. He moved his face closer until her lips were against his, then he shifted again and moved his lips against hers.

Her mouth fit perfectly against his. She hesitated briefly, then started kissing him back.

She must have had no idea how long he'd waited to kiss her. How he hadn't heard any conversation and barely tasted the food. If she knew even half of his longing to kiss her, she'd have either run away from him, scared, or . . .

He tried to block his thoughts out of his mind and think of nothing other than the kiss. Enjoy the moment. Ignore the guilt creeping up. He couldn't let her get too interested in him. She'd only feel hurt or angry when she realized that he was about to move away. He couldn't bear to be the source of her pain.

Long-distance relationships never worked.

He kept his lips pressed to hers, trying to memorize every detail of their kiss. She kissed him back with an equal sense of urgency as if she might feel the same way. But she couldn't care for him as much as he cared for her. She had been clear from the beginning. Their relationship wasn't based on real feelings. She only saw him as a solution to her problem, not a potential partner.

He needed to remember that.

A loud sound—feedback from a microphone and speaker —pierced the air. Emily jerked back. Bill held his breath but a low moan escaped. He raised his eyes to look at Emily, but she faced the dance floor, face paler than he thought possible, like she'd seen a ghost.

He should have known better than to kiss her like that in a room full of people. Next time, he'd have to take her out to the deck, find a private corner, and kiss her for as long as she'd allow. And then convince her to kiss him again.

He ran his finger over the side of her cheek, letting them come to a rest at her chin as she turned her head towards him and leaned into his hand. Her eyes were filled with something. Pain, or hurt? Maybe it was the music in the air, or her kiss, but he needed to erase away the sadness. "You can tell me what's bothering you. I know it's not easy for you to be here."

"I'm fine. It's just that this isn't how I expected the day to be. Anyway, we don't need to talk about my feelings. We can talk about something else." She broke eye contact, shifting her gaze slightly lower.

"You don't have to hide things from me." He applied slight pressure to her chin, tilting her face until she met his gaze again.

"What about you? Are you hiding anything?"

"No." He ignored the guilty twinge, telling him that he should tell her everything. About his PTSD, and about his family. She already guessed that he had PTSD. All he had to do was admit that she was right. But he couldn't. The last woman who knew about it turned her back on him because she couldn't handle his truth. And Emily had no idea about his family. His obligations. The reason why they could never be together. But she wasn't expecting them to date again after this weekend ended. There was no reason to burden her with his pain.

She tried to look away again, but this time he held her chin and brought her face closer to his. Her eyes were filled with mistrust, as though she knew he was holding something back.

"Why do you care about me? And why have you been the perfect boyfriend this weekend? Why are you here?" Her voice came out quietly, hesitantly, full of mistrust.

"You needed me." And he knew in that moment that he'd do more than take her away for the weekend to make her happy, if he didn't have other responsibilities tying him down.

Her eyes widened and she frowned. "I don't need anyone."

"I didn't mean--"

"I can handle things on my own."

"I didn't--"

"I'm not as naive as I used to be. I'm not going to fall for--"

"Emily, I'm not Ethan." He wanted to shout those words, but restrained himself and spoke calmly and evenly, yet sternly. Emily froze, shocked as if he'd yelled. He fought the urge to back down, but she needed to hear this. "He was never good enough for you. You should date again. You deserve someone better."

She stared at him for a moment, while his words sunk in. "Someone like you?" Emily's voice was sarcastic, but he heard the pain and vulnerability buried beneath the tone.

He stared into her eyes, wanting to ignore the doubt in her voice and let her know that, yes, she should be with him. That he would treat her better than any other man could. That she would be the center of his world. That he would spend all day, every day, trying to make her happier than she was the day before. But he couldn't. "My life is complicated. I can't commit to anyone right now."

The pain in her eyes was immediate. "I never asked you for a commitment. I'm fine without you or anyone."

A loud cheer rose from the dance floor, preventing Bill from saying else. Veronica's voice rang out over the speaker system. "All the single ladies, up front for the bouquet toss!"

Emily crossed her arms and sank lower in her chair. "Don't worry, Bill. I'm not going to go up there and catch the bouquet. You don't have to worry that I'll trap you into a relationship or --"

"Emily!" Veronica's voice shot out from the speakers again. She stood in the middle of the dancefloor, rotating slowly with the microphone held up to her face, scanning the guests in the room. "Emily, where are you? I have a whole speech prepared and if you don't come out here now, we can't do the bouquet toss. Where are you?" Veronica's voice rose higher and higher as she spoke.

Emily muttered something indecipherable under her breath.

Bill tried to ignore the impulse to pick Emily up and carry her out of the room, to somewhere far away from the dance floor. "Are we doing this? Are we engaged?"

"No. I won't lie." She held her hand up to her face, shielding herself from everyone on the dance floor.

"You have to let me do something." The hairs on the back of Bill's neck rose as the crowd on the dance floor grew larger.

Someone's voice broke out from the crowd. "I see her! She's over there! Table six!"

A few beads of sweat broke out over Bill's forehead as too many people turned to look at their table.

Veronica shrieked into the microphone again. "Emily, why didn't you say something? Come here! No, wait, I'll go there." Veronica took three steps towards Emily before the microphone cord stopped her. She contorted her face into a pout. "Ugh. Emily, you'll have to come up here for the bouquet toss. All the single ladies!"

The chatter in the reception hall lowered. Bill looked around for Ethan. Someone needed to put a stop to this, whatever it was.

"She's not single," he yelled, ensuring that his voice was heard over the crowd.

"She'd not married yet! That means she's single!" Veronica chirped into the microphone, smiling. Several of the bridesmaids cheered along and waved wildly for Emily to come up to the font.

He hesitated for only a second, then looked to Emily. How upset would she be if he announced that they were engaged?

As if she knew what he was going to say, Emily shook her head and stood up. "I don't need you to lie for me. Maybe I'll catch the bouquet and it will give me good luck. After all, I should get out there and start dating again, right?"

Bill reached out to stop her from walking away, but she was already out of his reach. He didn't want her to leave his side, not after looking at him with so much pain and hurt. And he'd been the cause of some of that pain.

Veronica chanted Emily's name as she approached the dance floor, and the chant spread like wildfire.

Bill scanned the room and saw Ethan standing near the exit. He gave Bill a smug, drunken smirk.

Bill made up his mind. Emily was his, at least for a few more hours, and he wouldn't let her face this alone.

"Everyone, quiet, please! I have something to say!" Veronica had a huge grin plastered across her face as she spoke into the microphone, now standing next to Emily on the dance floor. Either Veronica was ignoring Emily's fake smile, or she didn't care that Emily looked like she was walking in a room full of venomous snakes.

Bill tried to focus on Emily and block out the dread washing over him as people crowded around the room. He needed to keep his PTSD symptoms under control. For Emily.

Veronica was still talking. "I know it's not normal for brides to make a speech on their wedding day . . ." She scanned the room for Ethan and blew him a kiss, which made a few of the guests clap. "But many people might not know just how amazing Emily has been to Ethan and me." Veronica's voice lowered to a fake whisper. "She actually used to date Ethan"—her voice returned to her normal volume—"until Ethan and I met and fell in love. We had to keep our love a secret for the longest time, out of respect to Emily. But eventually, Emily found out how madly in love we were. She found out that Ethan had wanted to end their relationship for over a year but couldn't bring himself to break her heart. I don't know how many times he told me that Emily wouldn't be able to survive losing him. She never realized that his heart belonged to me."

Bill ran his hand through his hair and looked back to where he last saw Ethan, but he was gone. Every muscle in his chest and arms tensed, ready for battle. But there was no clear enemy, just a crowded room blocking his path to Emily.

He nudged his way past the wedding guests toward the edge of the dance floor while Veronica kept talking.

"Once Emily found out we were in love, she let Ethan go. Well, not without a fight." Veronica took a dramatic pause and chuckled. "Em, remember how mad you were the night you crashed Ethan's car? You still owe him the last payment for the repairs, by the way." She chuckled again, along with several other guests.

Emily still smiled at the crowd, and said nothing. Her smile didn't reach her eyes.

He recognized the emotions on her face. He'd seen that forced expression on the faces of patients and their families when they were given bad news—a combination of shock, hopelessness, and a last-ditch effort at self-preservation before falling apart.

He took one step onto the dance floor when a firm hand pressed down on his shoulder. He jerked away, fighting every urge to throw out a punch.

Ethan and Sam looked at him, wearing identical sneers. In that moment, Bill didn't care if Ethan was the groom. He'd make him pay if he hurt Emily again. "End this, Ethan."

"Take one more step toward my bride and you'll regret it."

"Are you threatening me?" Bill stood up tall, towering over Ethan, hoping he'd say yes so he'd have the chance to hit him and give him an ounce of the pain that Emily experienced at Ethan's hands.

Ethan merely shook his head. "Calm down. This is my wedding. I'm not going to fight you. But that doesn't mean I won't make my own speech about Emily. So don't mess with me." The evil look in his eye showed that he wasn't bluffing.

Bill jerked his gaze back to Veronica, who still rambled on into the microphone.

"—to formally thank Emily for eventually giving up on her dream of marriage so that Ethan and I could finally be together. By giving you my bouquet, I hope that some of my good luck will spread to you and that, one day, you'll know what true love feels like." Veronica handed her microphone to one of the women standing next to her and turned back to Emily, bouquet stretched out while guests clapped and cheered.

"Ethan, I swear, if you say anything to Emily, you'll have to cancel your honeymoon." Bill strained to keep his fist from connecting with Ethan's smug face.

The band started playing a lively rift and the women spread out over the dance floor, joined by the men who had waited on the sidelines during the bouquet toss. Bill tore his attention away from Ethan long enough to look back at Emily. The spot where she had stood moments ago was empty.

Bill started scanning the room. The shifting crowd made the hairs on the back of his neck stand on end, and his chest grew tight. There were too many people moving around on all sides. He couldn't keep track of everyone. A trickle of sweat ran down the side of his face.

Fear started taking over his body. He fought the pressure in his chest and tried to stay focused. He scanned the room again. Ethan was also out of sight. He couldn't see Ethan, and he couldn't see Emily. He needed to find her, and needed to get her out of this room. He needed to get himself out of this room and to somewhere secure.

His feet started moving on their own, taking him to the center of the dance floor, not caring how many dancing couples he bumped into along the way. He pushed his way through, but people were everywhere, on all sides. And there was no sign of Emily.

He twisted his head to the left, and caught sight of Sam. He didn't trust Sam. He didn't trust any friend of Ethan's. He couldn't see who Sam was talking to. There were too many people standing between them.

Bill maneuvered his way through the crowd to get closer to Sam. If he found Sam, he might find Ethan. Veronica too, if he was lucky. If he found Ethan, he'd know that Emily was safe, for a moment.

The crowd thinned in front of him, and he caught a glimpse of Emily's auburn hair. That creep, Sam, stood too close to her, talking to her with a smirk that Bill didn't like. No one was allowed to look at Emily like that. Bill pushed his way harder through the crowd. He needed to get to Emily and get her away from Sam.

A loud thud of skin hitting skin pierced the air, followed by an even louder gasp from the crowd. Sam's head jerked back. Someone clutched at Bill's arm, but he ignored it. His attention immediately went back to Emily.

Emily spun around, cupping her right hand in her left. Her eyes were full of fire. Sam stood next to her, bent over slightly and holding his jaw. She almost instantly spotted Bill.

Bill froze under the impact of her gaze, trying to take in what happened. His feet stopped working. His heart stopped too. She was safe.

Someone pushed up against his side, but he didn't move or break eye contact with Emily. A woman standing next to him spoke close to his ear. "She punched Sam."

A sense of pride washed over him. Her hand was going to ache tonight, but she did it. She stood up for herself.

She took a few unsteady steps towards Bill, then stopped. The color drained from her cheeks.

"How could you?" She broke eye contact with him and looked at his side.

He couldn't tear his eyes away from her. "Emily? Are you ok?" He didn't want to rush up to her and spook her, even though every ounce of him wanted to pick her up in his arms and carry her far away. He wasn't going to force himself into her personal space like Sam just did.

She slowly shook her head. "You promised." Her voice came out quietly, strained, and just loud enough for Bill to hear.

He took a step forward. As he did, he felt the pressure increase on his arm. He looked over and realized the newest source of Emily's pain. Clare had her arm wrapped around his.

He shook his hand to free himself but Clare held on tightly.

"Bill, let's get out of here. Everyone is staring at us." Clare was tall enough to whisper in his ear without stretching.

"Emily, it's not what you think."

Emily's expression was enough to stop him from saying anything else. "I should have known better. I should have realized . . . I . . ." her voice trailed off without finishing her sentence.

Bill took another step to her and tried to shake Clare off of his arm. She kept a firm grip and stepped forward with him.

"Come on, Bill." Clare's voice came out as a whine. "She's crazy and violent. Let's get away from all this. I want to see your dance moves." She tugged his arm but he didn't move.

Emily spoke directly to Bill, ignoring Clare. "Of course

you'd say that. They all say that. 'It's not what you think.' Do you think I'm that stupid?"

Clare released one of her hands from his arm and ran it over his chest as Emily spoke. Bill grasped Clare's hand and tried to break away.

It took every ounce of self-discipline to stay in control. There was no way to keep an eye on everything happening in the room. People stood around him on all sides, blocking the path to any exit. And Clare's hand running over his chest made him want to scream.

He needed to get Emily out of there as fast as possible. He needed to get her somewhere safe and secure. He couldn't be in that room for much longer, but he couldn't leave without her.

He brushed aside Clare's hand one last time and stepped away from her.

Sam and Ethan chose the wrong moment to appear and block his path.

"Move." Bill's body automatically prepared for an attack.

Ethan held up his hand and smirked. "Easy, man. We're just having fun."

"Leave Emily out of this."

Sam looked back at Emily. "Don't want to. And she owes me an apology."

"She owes you nothing."

"This is between Emily and me. Stay out of it," Sam said.

Bill stepped forward, his body moving into a fighting stance.

Sam puffed out his chest and raised his chin. "Get out of here, Bill."

Bill couldn't help himself. He raised his fist and drew it back. "Last warning, Sam. I throw a harder punch than Emily."

Sam flinched slightly. Bill waited without lowering his

fist. He looked away for a second to seek out Emily, but she wasn't standing where he last saw her.

He lowered his fist slightly and started scanning the room. If anyone else had their hands on her, there would be a price to pay.

Something hard hit his stomach, and the air rushed out of his lungs. He doubled over, gasping for breath. He raised his eyes to see Sam standing in front of him, fists raised, bouncing on his feet like he was ready to fight. His stance was weak. Bill could take him out in under a minute. He looked like an overly excited puppy who wanted to play.

Ethan watched him warily. Judging by the strength of Sam's sucker punch, Bill could take them both.

But it wasn't worth it. He needed to find Emily.

He glared at Sam. "This is your last warning. Leave Emily alone."

He turned and walked out of the reception hall.

EMILY

A blast of wind took away her breath as she walked through the door to the boat's large deck. She glanced over her shoulder, but no one followed. A few curious eyes met hers, but most of the guests faced the dance floor. She didn't even want to imagine what was happening between Sam, Ethan, and Bill. As soon as Sam and Ethan stepped between her and Bill, she saw her chance for escape and took it. She wanted to be away from all of them.

He had made a promise and she believed him. That was her problem. She always wanted to believe the best in people. She always thought that people would make the right decision in the end.

But he hadn't.

She gave him the benefit of the doubt. She even managed to convince herself that he always looked around the room at everyone in it because he had PTSD and didn't feel safe. She lied to herself and made up excuses for him.

Now she felt like a fool.

She pulled her phone out of her purse and called Ashley.

No answer. She tried Theresa next. She answered on the second ring.

"Theresa, I just punched someone." Emily cringed as she spoke. She was officially freaking out.

"Emily?"

"I'm on the boat, and I just punched this guy named Sam, and the whole situation got out of control."

"Are you ok?"

"My hand hurts like crazy. I don't know if I broke something or not."

"What did he do to you? Do I need to call the cops? Are you safe?" Theresa's voice sounded strained over the phone.

Emily cringed again. "No, I'm fine. I mean, I'm safe. I'm not fine, though. I'm freaking out. Do you think they'll arrest me for punching Sam? I could be charged with assault."

"Emily, focus." Theresa's voice lost her usual upbeat tone. "You won't get charged with assault. Just tell me what happened."

Emily glanced around. A small group of people meandered onto the deck and walked her way. She turned. "I have to find somewhere quiet. This boat is too small. There's got to be somewhere to hide."

"Are you hiding from the guy you punched?"

"Sam? No, I need to hide from Bill. And everyone else."

"You have to tell me what happened."

"Hang on a minute." A couple stood up and walked away from a bench halfway down the boat. Emily grabbed the boat railing for stability and walked unsteadily to the bench as the waves rocking the boat and her high heels threatened to make her fall. "Veronica made this huge embarrassing speech before handing me the bouquet. Then Ethan threw the garter to Sam, and we were supposed to have a special dance together. Honestly, I used to think Sam was a decent guy. He called me a few times after Ethan and I broke up. He was nice at first. But after he asked me out a few times and I kept turning him down, he got jealous and mean."

"Why did you punch him?"

"We started dancing but he wouldn't let me go. I warned him and he laughed. So I punched him."

Theresa let out a loud breath. "I hate violence, but in this situation, he deserved it. I never thought you would have done that. I'm glad you stuck up for yourself."

A wave of relief washed over Emily. "The weird thing is that I'm glad too. I never hit a guy before, or anyone else. I feel good. My hand doesn't even hurt anymore."

"It will probably hurt again later. But for now, enjoy the adrenaline rush."

"Is this why people get into fights? Does it always feel this good after you win?" Emily studied her hand for bruising.

"Probably. But instead of taking up street fighting, you should come to my kickboxing class with me."

Theresa had mentioned her class before, but Emily thought she was crazy for even suggesting it. "Sign me up. If it feels this good, I'll do it."

"Great. Where was Bill for all of this?"

"I'm done with him. He was wrapped around another woman the entire time Sam tried to get me to dance with him. They're probably making out somewhere on the boat now."

"Jerk. Don't worry about him anymore. I found the perfect guys for you."

"What?"

"On the dating app. I found seven guys so far. They are all hot. Any one of them could be your soulmate."

Emily chewed her lip. "Seven guys?

"That's only the start. I sent you an email with your login information. Log in and check it now."

"Now?"

"If you don't take the next step, you'll never actually start dating again."

Emily moved the phone from her ear and tapped the screen a few times. A page with men's faces appeared. Each man looked like he could be a toothpaste model. One guy was blond, another had on dark sunglasses and looked like he was in the middle of the woods. A third guy bore a remarkable appearance to Bill, but wasn't him. She moved the phone back to her ear. "Want to meet for coffee tomorrow afternoon and help me pick out some dates?"

"Sounds great! I'm so excited! We can go shopping again and get some really cute dresses. Can you walk in really high heels? Higher than the ones you bought for the wedding? It doesn't matter, I can teach you. This is going to be so fun!"

Emily rolled her eyes. She still wasn't used to Theresa's enthusiasm, but it was contagious. "Thanks for setting up my online dating profile."

"Byeee!" Theresa drew out the word as Emily hung up.

Things were going to be alright. Even better than alright. It was like something burst loose in her when she punched Sam. She didn't need to put up with guys who didn't know how to treat her well. She didn't need to date men who thought they were better than her. She was going to take charge of her dating life instead of sitting on the sidelines, waiting for someone to notice her.

She stood up and turned around.

Bill stared at her.

Her phone fell from her hand, landing on the boat's deck with a loud thud. How much had he heard?

He slowly bent over and picked up her phone without breaking eye contact. He rose back to his full height, crossing his arms and looking taller than ever. "Sit down."

EMILY

Emily crossed her arms, not ready to back down to anyone. "I'm not a dog. I don't sit on command." She turned around and started to walk.

He spoke louder. "I have your phone."

She flinched and stopped. She lifted her uninjured hand and held it out to her side, palm facing upwards, without looking back at him or saying anything. "Give it back."

"I'm not a dog. I don't fetch on command," he said, echoing her words.

Even without looking at him, Emily could hear that half-smirk in his voice. The sly curve of his lip that made her skin tingle.

"Dogs fetch after you throw something. I didn't throw my phone," she said, moving her hand impatiently behind her back, refusing to turn and look at him.

She heard him take a few quiet steps in her direction. She stretched her opened palm farther behind her.

Something shockingly cold contacted her hand.

She jerked her hand away and turned around, almost smashing right into his chest.

"Give me my phone." She lowered her eyes to look at his chest instead of his face.

He held an ice pack in front of her.

"I don't want ice. I want my phone." She held out her left hand between them again, palm facing up.

"Take the ice. Your hand is probably swelling up as we speak." His voice was firm.

She moved her right hand behind her back so he couldn't see it. "That's my problem, not yours."

He groaned and stepped back. "Fine." He walked to the same bench she had been sitting on and sat down, facing the lake, and placed the ice pack on the seat next to him. He reached into his jacket pocket and pulled out her phone.

Her eyes narrowed. "Give me back my phone."

He either didn't hear her or actually ignored her. She narrowed her eyes as his fingers flicked over the screen. He'd never guess her passcode.

She turned to walk away. She'd just get her phone later. Except how would she get back to the hotel without her phone? She had money in her wallet, which was still in her purse. But she needed the phone to order a ride share to get back to the hotel. Not to mention that she was going to check out of the hotel as soon as she packed up her suitcase and secured a rental car. And in order to get a rental car, she needed her phone.

Bill was obviously baiting her. What was his problem? Was he really that much of a playboy that he needed to chase one woman after another and drive women crazy when they tried to walk away? Was this a game to him?

She turned around again. She was going to make herself seasick if she kept changing her mind and turning around, but she wouldn't lose this battle. If she walked up quietly, she could sneak behind him and snatch her phone out of her hand. Then he'd have nothing to hold over her, and there'd be no more reason to talk to him again.

She made it to the back of the bench and held her breath. One quick grab and the phone would be hers again. She glanced at her right hand. It was swollen but didn't hurt. It was still a better option than trying to snatch the phone with her left hand.

She reached forward quickly and brushed her hand against the phone. A bolt of pain shot through her hand and up her arm. She tried to pull back but Bill's hand was already wrapped around her arm, near her elbow. "Let go!"

He didn't even turn around to look at her. He used his free hand to tuck her phone back into the inside pocket of his suit jacket and picked up the ice pack. He adjusted his grip on her arm so he could see her hand.

She stopped struggling and gritted her teeth again. He turned her hand over and looked at her knuckles, where the swelling was the worst. After he looked at it long enough, he covered her hand with the ice pack.

She let out a quiet hiss as the ice contacted her skin. After a few seconds, the cold sensation started to feel good.

"Come sit down." Bill still didn't look at her.

She hesitated. "I'm not a dog." Even to her own ears, she didn't sound as stern as she had earlier. She frowned and tried again. "I want my phone."

"You'll get your phone. After you make me a promise."

That demand lit the fire in her again. "I don't owe you anything!"

"No, you don't."

Emily tried to move her injured hand out of his grasp again, but his grip around her wrist was like steel. She considered her choices briefly and then walked around the bench. He adjusted his grip as she moved so that she could sit in the empty space next to him. As soon as she sat, she regretted the choice. The bench was short and his shoulders were broad. Even with her side pressed up to the railing at the side of the bench, the length of his body pressed against hers.

She tugged her arm again.

"Stop pulling so much. You need to ice your hand."

"I can hold ice against my own hand without any help." She quickly looked forward as his head turned to hers. She could handle the view of the lake better than the view of his eyes.

He inhaled like he was going to say something, then let the breath out without talking.

Emily tried to focus on following the path of a bird flying towards the edge of the lake. "How did you know I was here?"

"I walked around the deck of the boat until I found you."

"I meant, how did you know I was behind you just now? When I tried to get my phone back?"

He shrugged. "Military training."

She grunted. "So you *were* in the military."

"You knew that. Ethan told you."

"I shouldn't have found it out from Ethan."

He leaned in closer to her. She used every ounce of restraint to keep her eyes locked on the trees on the shore of the lake. "I haven't lied to you."

She couldn't take it any longer. She twisted on the bench to face him and gave her arm another tug. He barely moved but kept her hand locked in his. "Our entire relationship has been a lie. You aren't my boyfriend. You aren't here because you love me. You aren't going to stay with me after this weekend is over." She had trouble keeping quiet enough to avoid attracting attention, but she didn't care. "I want my phone back."

He shifted his grasp on her arm, making her lean in closer

to him. His face was inches away. A shadow passed over his eyes. "So you can start messaging all those guys on that dating app? Line up the next guy to date once you're done with me?"

She inhaled deeply. "You broke into my phone?"

"You should have a better passcode. 1234 is an easy guess for anyone."

"Why shouldn't I start looking for someone to date? You already found your next girlfriend. And you promised not to hit on any other women today." She blinked hard.

"What are you talking about?"

"Don't pretend that I didn't see Clare running her hand up and down your chest when Sam trapped me on the dance floor."

He looked down and muttered something quietly. "Emily, that whole situation was nothing more than Ethan and Sam trying to get back at me."

"That's not true."

"Em, listen to me, please. If I had known this was Ethan's wedding, I wouldn't have come. I would have found another way to help you. But I found out too late. Ethan blames me for getting kicked out of the military. I turned him in after he did something illegal. I thought he was just going to try to hurt me today. I never thought he'd try to hurt me through you."

"That doesn't make sense. He was trying to embarrass me." Emily's eyes started to sting, and she blinked harder than before.

"It does make sense. Clare is Sam's sister. She screamed at Sam after you left. Ethan and Sam planned to break us up today, and Clare was supposed to help."

Emily thought over his words. He might have told the truth, or he might have just told a lie in order to trick her. "Don't act like I'm stupid. Even if that was true, how do you explain the texts you got this weekend? Julie seemed eager to see you again. And then there was the other number who wanted to meet up for drinks." She lifted her chin slightly. "Don't deny that you already have dinner reservations for next weekend with another woman. Maybe Clare was playing along with a plot to break us up. Are you going to tell me that Ethan and Sam set you up with all these other women too?"

A muscle in Bill's neck started twitching. "Em, I can explain all of that. I—"

Emily shook her head. "Don't explain anything. We aren't even dating. You owe me nothing. But maybe I can guess, just for fun. Let's see . . ." Emily tilted her head and frowned. "You were going to say that one of the women was your sister, or maybe a cousin. And that another one was just a friend from work. Maybe even that you were going to meet up with a group of people from work, and she was just the one in charge of making plans."

Bill swallowed hard, looking like a deer caught in head-lights. She guessed right. It felt horrible, though. She didn't feel an ounce of satisfaction.

"Bill, I want my phone back."

Her words wiped the stare from his face. His eyes darkened. "Don't go on that dating app, Emily. Please."

"It's not your concern."

He growled quietly. "Don't you understand? You've driven me crazy for weeks. Ever since I met you, I couldn't stop thinking about you. Each time I see you, I can't think straight. Ask Ashley or her boyfriend. They know how I feel. You've taken over my thoughts. I'll go crazy if you start dating someone else."

Emily's mouth dropped open. This was really too much. What was he thinking?

The boat lurched gently and Emily glanced out over the

railing. They were docked. A voice came over the speaker, announcing that all guests should leave the boat.

"Emily?"

She looked back at him. He looked pained. "You can't possibly expect me to believe that. You couldn't stop looking around the room at other women each time we met up last week." She couldn't breathe or tear her eyes away from his.

He looked at her swollen hand and adjusted the ice before he spoke. "You were right earlier when you guessed that I had PTSD. It's true. I can't comfortably sit in a room without constantly looking around, making sure nothing bad is about to happen. I need to know where all the exits are. I had to drive here because I can't be relaxed in the car if anyone else drives. I didn't admit it when you asked because you worked so hard to convince that old couple to switch seats. I didn't want to put you through that again at another table." He paused and then added, quietly, "I didn't want you to think I'm weak."

She studied his eyes for a minute. He looked and sounded sincere. "I don't know what to think anymore."

"Don't think. Just believe me."

She searched his eyes for an answer. Any answer.

Another announcement from the speaker jolted her out of her thoughts.

"Bill, I want my phone."

He sighed. He released his hold on her hand and wrist, making her skin ache with longing for him to touch her again. "Take it."

She reached tentatively for his jacket, maintaining eye contact. She couldn't look away, even if she tried. Her right hand was throbbing now that there was no ice on it, so she reached inside his jacket with her left hand. She closed her hand around her phone and pulled it out.

"Bill . . ."

"Come back to the hotel with me. We can talk about anything. I'll tell you everything you want to know."

She swallowed hard and nodded once. He stood up immediately and held his hand out to her. Emily paused, then reached for her purse to put her phone away before she lost it again. As soon as she glanced down, she realized she had a missed text.

I need you. This can't wait. Come here as soon as you can.

She caught her breath and looked at the sender. Julie.

Emily narrowed her eyes. She didn't know anyone named Julie. Except . . .

"Bill, I grabbed the wrong phone." She stood up and held it out to him. "Give me my phone."

His eyes narrowed as he reached into his jacket and pulled out another phone from the same pocket. He traded phones with her and then looked at his screen. His lips moved silently as he read.

"Emily, let me explain this."

Emily turned around and started walking to the exit. "I don't need to hear anything." Hadn't she put up with enough lying from Ethan? And she and Bill never even really dated. If they never dated, he was free to date whomever else he wanted.

"She's my sister! Look, I have proof." He caught up to her and held out his phone. "See? Here's a picture of us together."

She glanced down involuntarily and saw a picture of Bill posing with a gorgeous woman. "You two look nothing alike."

"I'm adopted."

She narrowed her eyes at him again. "Give it up, Bill. There's no reason to lie. You can date anyone you want. I'll do the same."

"Emily . . ." He glanced down at his phone again.

Emily looked up ahead and saw her parents in line to get

off the boat. She took a few quick steps, darting in between other guests who were lining up.

Her parents looked up in surprise when they saw her. Her mom spoke first. "Emily, where have you been? We've been looking for you."

Emily shook her head. "I'll explain later." She turned to her dad. "Can you give me a ride to the hotel? I need to pack my bags. I'm leaving tonight."

28

EMILY

Emily rubbed her ear and paced the hotel room, still wearing her dress and heels from the reception. She could change after she got the rental car and far away from Bill. "Say that again?" she spoke into her phone.

The clerk on the other line repeated, "We don't have any cars available for one-way rentals tonight. But we have a fifteen-passenger van."

"I don't even know how to drive a van that large. Do I need a special license?"

She heard a computer keyboard clicking on the other end of the line before he responded. "No."

She stopped pacing and threw some clothes in her suitcase. She'd fold them later, after she was safely away from Bill. "Fine. How much?"

He clicked some more keys before responding.

The number made her wince. "I'll take it."

She went into the bathroom and grabbed her toothbrush and makeup bag, tossing them on top of the tossed clothes in her suitcase. She surveyed the room. If she left anything else there, it was just the cost of avoiding Bill.

"Do you guys do that thing where you'll pick me up and drive me to the rental agency, or do I need to get a ride there myself?" She waited for the clicking of keys again. This clerk couldn't answer any questions without typing first.

She squashed the suitcase down and fought with the zipper. Finally, it closed. She turned it upright and wheeled to the door. She wouldn't need the room key anymore. She left it on the table by the door and left the room.

She could still hear the clerk typing into his computer through the phone. "Excuse me? I just need to know if I can get picked up by your agency or if I need to hire a car to get there."

More keyboard clicks. She stopped at the elevator. If this call went on any longer, she'd go crazy.

"Just a moment while I look up something in our system, please."

She stepped into the elevator and pressed the button for the lobby. The door closed and, within seconds, her phone beeped in her ear. Call dropped.

She stomped her foot. She actually stomped it on the floor. She never actually saw someone get mad enough to do that, except preschool children. She should have known better. She should have known that coming to this wedding would bring out the worst in her. She definitely should have stayed far away from Bill.

She glanced at the ceiling of the elevator just in case there was a security camera. She didn't need anyone, even a stranger, seeing her lash out like that.

The doors opened to the lobby, and she glanced around before stepping out. She didn't see anyone she recognized. They were probably at the after-party she'd heard about. At least no one invited her to go there.

She walked through the empty lobby and sat in a chair next to the large windows overlooking the lake. The final rays of sunlight shone across the water. It looked so peaceful. On any other day, she'd love nothing more than to curl up in this chair, reading a good book or sharing a glass of wine with a gorgeous guy. Not today.

Today, she needed to finish booking that rental car and get back to her apartment. If she could leave within the next hour, she could be home by midnight. She picked up her phone to call the agency again.

The screen flickered on briefly then went black. She pressed the power button. She pressed it again. She shook her phone. The stupid phone had a dead battery.

That was fine. She could deal with a dead battery. Her charger was in her suitcase, and there was an open outlet two chairs over. She grabbed her bag and changed seats. Her feet were killing her, and her hand was swollen to twice its normal size now, but she just needed to make it through the next twenty minutes. She'd change clothes, put on sneakers, and find ice after she had the keys to the rental car.

She checked her suitcase and then checked it again. Her charger wasn't in its normal pocket in her suitcase. It wasn't under her makeup bags either. She ran her hand through the clothes, pushing them around, but the charger wasn't there either.

She froze and groaned. She could clearly remember where she last saw her charger. She left it in Bill's car earlier that afternoon, when they drove to the wedding. The poor reception on the lake meant that her battery might drain quickly, and she wanted to be able to charge her phone in case they went somewhere after the reception. She regretted that decision now.

She could deal with a dead phone and no charger, though. Hotels always had chargers available for guests to borrow. She could just borrow one and charge her phone. In twenty-five minutes, she'd have the keys to a fifteen-passenger van and be on her way back to her hotel.

Pushing down on the lid of her suitcase again, she was able to force the zipper closed. Then she stood up and tried to ignore the protest from the blister on her foot. At this point, who would care if she wore a fancy dress with sneakers? But she needed that car.

She walked up to the front desk and put on her largest smile for the clerk. "Hello, my phone is dead and I don't have my charger. Do you have one I can borrow?"

She shouldn't have even bothered to smile. The man behind the counter didn't even look up at her. "We have phone chargers for sale. Forty dollars.."

Her jaw dropped open. She could buy a charger from the store for a fraction of that price. "Fine. I'll take it." She told him her type of phone and he walked into a back room. He emerged a minute later with a phone charger.

"Forty dollars."

She automatically reached for her purse at her side, then froze. "I left my purse in my room."

"I'll keep the charger up here until you get back with the money."

"Can you charge it to my room? Add it to the bill?" She could at least plug her phone in while she went back to the room to get her purse.

"What room is that?"

"1002."

He looked at his computer screen and typed. Emily did everything she could not to roll her eyes. Seriously, was tonight the night that no one could help her without first typing into a computer?

She put her hand to the side of her face to block her view of the front entrance. The last thing she needed was for Bill to walk in and notice her standing up there.

The clerk looked at her. "Your name?"

"Emily."

"ID?"

"It's in the room."

"I can't charge it to the room without proof of identification."

Emily's shoulders tensed and she forced out another smile. "Fine. I'll be back in five minutes."

He looked at her with a bored expression. "Ok."

She turned around and dragged her suitcase to the elevator. For the first time, she felt pangs of regret over punching Sam. Her hand hurt too much to use it to pull her suitcase, but it was awkward to pull it with her left hand.

But it didn't matter. She'd have the keys for the rental car in thirty minutes. Or at least in under an hour. She could survive that long.

She stood in the elevator and pressed the button for the tenth floor. The doors closed, then opened again to the lobby. She pressed the button again. The same thing happened. She went to press it the third time when she remembered that she needed the room key to operate the elevator.

She'd left the room key in the hotel room.

This was just getting ridiculous. There had to be a hidden camera somewhere around here. She couldn't possibly be this disorganized to get herself locked out of the hotel room, with no money or wallet, and a non-functioning phone.

She tried not to limp as she ambled back to the front desk. She should never have let Theresa talk her into buying these shoes. She pasted on another smile as the clerk gave her the same bored look.

"Back already? Can I see your ID?"

"Well, that's the problem. I left my hotel key in the room with my ID."

He clicked a few keys on the keyboard. "It says here that two keys were requested for that room."

"Yes. But I don't know where the other person is with that key, and I'm actually trying to avoid him."

"I suggest you contact the other guest in that room so you can use their key."

"I can't. I'm trying to avoid him. And my phone is dead."

He looked at her, clearly still bored.

"Do you have a charger I can borrow for five minutes? Just enough to turn on my phone again?"

"I can sell you this charger for forty dollars."

She looked down at the counter and counted to five. "I don't have any money. It's in the room with my charger, my ID, and my room key. If you can make a key, you can walk in there with me and I'll show you my ID."

"We have a policy against allowing unauthorized individuals into hotel rooms. Especially for the rooms on the executive floor."

Emily squeezed her hand and instantly regretted it. She let out a quiet hiss. "I'm not unauthorized. I just locked myself out of the room."

He shrugged and said nothing.

Emily gave him one last glance before she turned around and stalked back to the empty chairs in the lobby.

She could handle this. All she had to do was figure out a way to get back to the room. Or find someone she knew who would let her borrow a charger.

She smiled. Her parents were at the hotel! They gave her a ride back after the reception, and they had the same model phone. They'd let her borrow a charger and probably even loan her the money for the rental car so she wouldn't have to get her purse tonight.

She just needed her driver's license.

Well, she could still figure this out. She could find her

parents, borrow a charger, sleep in their room tonight, and get a ride back to her apartment in the city tomorrow.

She just needed her keys so she could get into her apartment and her car.

She shook her head. She'd have time to figure out all the details later. She just needed to charge her phone first.

She scanned her brain, trying to remember which room her parents were in. Did they say room 802? Or 208? Maybe it was 228? No, that didn't sound right. The room number definitely had a number four in it.

She walked back up to the desk, her feet aching. She really hated these shoes. "Excuse me, can you tell me which room Cheryl and Don Sager are in?"

The clerk gave her an annoyed look this time. "No." He looked back at the computer.

"No?"

"We have a policy against releasing guest information without authorization."

"Can you call their room and ask them to come to the front desk to meet me?"

He picked up the phone and pressed a few numbers. Emily tried to peer over the counter to see what numbers he pressed, but he moved his hand to block her view. He placed the phone receiver to his ear for several seconds before returning it to its original position on the counter.

"No answer."

"Can you call back and leave a voicemail?"

"The voicemail isn't set up in that room. Or any room of the hotel. Hotel guests usually use their personal cell phones to contact other guests. Anything else?" He spoke in a tone that was the opposite of helpful.

Emily tried her best not to climb over the counter, run to the back office, and steal a charging cord for her phone.

"Where's the ladies' room? Or do I need to show you ID in order to use the bathroom?"

He stifled a yawn. "Around the corner, to the right."

She gave him a glare for good measure and limped around the corner, dragging her suitcase with her uninjured hand. She pushed the door open and walked into the lobby bathroom.

The bathroom was empty, luckily. She walked into the nearest one. Why were the bathroom stalls so small? She couldn't even get her suitcase in behind her. She tried the next stall, but it was the same size. The only large stall was locked with an out-of-order sign on the door.

She could handle this. She wasn't giving up yet. She put the suitcase on the floor and opened it, with one eye towards the door. The entire situation would look better once she was out of this backless dress and torture-device shoes. She reached her hand in and touched something wet and sticky.

She jerked her hand back. Something clear and gooey was all over the top of the clothes in her bag. She leaned closer, carefully, and sniffed. It had a light floral smell that she instantly recognized—her shampoo.

All the clothes on the top of her suitcase were covered. It must have leaked after she shoved everything back in when she couldn't find her charger. That meant that it had only leaked for about five minutes, but definitely not more than ten minutes. How could it have possibly soaked through so many clothes?

She pulled out one shirt after another, each one coated with shampoo. It had leaked everywhere, probably because she hadn't taken the time to actually fold the clothes and store them neatly. She'd never make that mistake in the future. She was also going to invest in that shampoo bar she saw advertised on the internet. Or maybe never wash her hair when she traveled.

At last, she pulled out some clothes from the very bottom of the suitcase that seemed to have survived the shampoo apocalypse. Her yoga pants were at least comfortable. She could definitely wear her sneakers with them and be comfortable for the drive home. But the shirt wasn't one she recognized or remembered packing.

It was grey, with a logo for a medical association's conference from two years ago. She never attended that conference. She furrowed her brow and held the shirt up to her face to smell it. The scent was unmistakable. Bill.

That man must have left his shirt on her side of the bed this morning as some type of joke after their late-night conversation. Well, the joke was on him now. He'd never get that shirt back because she didn't plan on ever talking to him again.

She rummaged around her suitcase one last time. There really was no other shirt to wear. She ground her teeth and went into the bathroom stall with the only available clean clothes.

Minutes later, she emerged from the lobby bathroom wearing yoga pants and Bill's shirt, with her hair tied up in a messy bun. Comfortable at last, as long as she could ignore the feeling of Bill's shirt against her skin and his unmistakable scent.

She marched over to a chair in the lobby that faced the main entrance and the main elevators. If her parents walked through the lobby, she'd see them in an instant. If Bill came through, she'd see him too. She'd be on her way to a rental car by early morning, which would leave her enough time to stop by the grocery store on the way to her apartment to pick up a pint of ice cream. Two pints. And maybe some chips and Chinese food takeout.

29

EMILY

A voice interrupted her dream.

"Ma'am, ma'am, umm. . . Hey you, wake up. You can't sleep here. I'm going to call security."

She groaned and peeled one eye open. Whoever was talking should really lower his voice and not disturb everyone around.

"You can't stay here. Either get a room or leave the property. Hotel policy."

She recognized that voice. That unhelpful front-desk clerk. And now he stood in front of her, staring.

She sat up and looked around the room, confused. She must have fallen asleep. "What time is it?"

"Ten. If you are going to stay here for the night, you need to book a room."

"Geez, give me a minute to wake up." She muttered under her breath and rubbed her eyes. "I have a room here, remember? I locked myself out and you won't let me in to get my purse."

He shrugged. "Hotel policy. If you don't leave now, I'll have security escort you out."

She stared at him. He was serious. He really was going to kick her out.

"Can I talk to the manager? Or someone else? I need to get back in my room or at least get my phone charged."

He shook his head. "No manager here tonight. You can talk to them in the morning."

"Where am I supposed to go until then?"

He reached for a walkie-talkie that she hadn't previously noticed in his hand.

"Wait, don't call security yet. Are you really going to kick me out? I have nowhere to go."

"Hotel policy."

"But you can bend the policy. You said there's no manager here tonight."

He didn't break eye contact as he raised the walkie-talkie to his face. The device beeped. "Security, can you—?"

"Wait!" Emily jumped up and yelled across the lobby. A familiar face just walked through the front door. "Bill! Bill! Over here!"

She didn't even care if anyone in the lobby stared at her. He was the only person at the moment who could keep her from spending the night sleeping under a tree, where she'd probably get eaten by a wolf or bear. Or, with her luck today, sprayed by a skunk.

He would help, right? Even if he was mad at her for running away from him on the boat, he couldn't be the type of man to leave her stranded. Unless she messed up worse than she thought when they broke up on the boat. But it wasn't an actual breakup, because they hadn't been actually dating. And who could blame her for being upset at him?

His face was blank as he walked across the lobby towards them.

"Bill, tell him." She spoke quickly and pointed to the hotel clerk. "Tell him that I have a room here. Tell him not to call security and kick me out."

Bill crossed his arms and studied her, running his eyes up and down her clothes. She looked down and winced. She still had his shirt on.

It didn't matter. She hadn't stolen it. Or at least, she didn't steal it on purpose. And he'd understand that she only put it on after the rest of her clothes got drenched with shampoo. She definitely wasn't wearing it because the scent made her feel safe and warm inside.

She pointed to the clerk again. "He's about to make me leave the hotel. Tell him that I'm staying here and give me your room key." She reached her hand out and regretted the movement instantly. She really needed to stop using her right hand until the swelling went down. The first signs of bruising marked her knuckles.

Bill didn't move. "Did you get my text?"

"My phone died."

He nodded once. "What are you doing in the lobby?"

"He won't give me an extra key to the room."

The clerk obviously wasn't pleased with this interaction. He pressed the button on the walkie-talkie again. "Security, hotel lobby, please. Need to escort someone off the premises."

"Wait!" Emily tried to keep from yelling at him. "Bill, you have to help me. Please."

Emily took a step towards Bill. He looked tired, with dark circles under his eyes. He also wasn't wearing the same clothes he had on earlier. He wore a pair of jeans and a faded t-shirt, similar to the one she wore. When did he have time to change his clothes? Did he pack a change of clothes to bring with him to the wedding? Or did he change when he met up with his so-called sister, Julie? He probably had lots of extra clothes at her place. No woman would send that type of text unless she was used to having the man show up at her place often.

She crossed her arms and lowered her voice. "Bill, you are free to date anyone you want. Just let me into the room so I can grab my purse and phone charger. I'll book a separate room and leave you alone."

That finally jolted Bill out of whatever state of mind he'd been in. He narrowed his eyes and looked at the clerk. "She's with me." He reached over, grabbed her suitcase handle, and started to walk towards the elevator without looking back at her.

Emily looked back at the clerk. "Happy? I wasn't lying. If you'd believed me and let me into that room, this whole situation would have been easier."

He shrugged. "Hotel policy." At least he turned around and walked away.

She turned back to look at Bill. He had gone around the corner, out of view. She shot off at a full run.

The elevator doors opened just as she rounded the corner. Bill stepped in and turned around, holding the door open for her.

She didn't dare slow down but ran full speed until she got into the elevator. She crashed right into him with a thud.

"Umph."

He looked down at her but didn't say anything as he wrapped his arms around her in a tight grip. He briefly broke eye contact as he reached around her, waved the hotel room key over the sensor, and pressed the button for the floor.

Emily wiggled to break away but he didn't budge. Of course, he'd remember how to use the elevator each time he got in it. He probably never forgot a hotel room key, never lost his wallet, never let his phone battery run out, and never got caught sleeping in a hotel lobby wearing his ex's clothes. Wait, he wasn't her ex-anything—just her ex-fake-boyfriend.

He let go of her when the elevator door opened on their floor. Once again, he walked out of the elevator, pulling her suitcase without looking back.

She followed him into their room. "Look, about your shirt . . ." She pulled the shirt away from her body as she spoke. "I didn't mean to—"

He interrupted her and held out his hand. "Phone?"

She reached into the pocket of her yoga pants and pulled it out, placing it in his hand. "I'll wash your shirt and give it back to you on Monday."

He walked to the bedroom and disappeared for a few minutes. She used that time to survey the room until she found her purse lying next to the chair in the sitting area. She picked it up and walked back to her suitcase, opening it carefully.

At least now she could go through the clothes more easily. There must be something in her suitcase that wasn't covered with shampoo. Anything.

Bill came back in the room, paused for a moment, and then walked over to the large chair. He sat down, leaned back, and stared directly at her.

She looked back at her suitcase and tried to focus. A pair of underwear was right on top. Not the sexy kind of underwear, but the comfortable kind. She shoved it under a shampoo-soaked shirt. "I was going to leave, but I locked my purse and wallet in here by mistake. My phone died in the hotel lobby, so I couldn't call anyone. That clerk thinks it's fun to watch other people suffer. He wouldn't let me buy a charger without any cash and wouldn't let me into our room without any ID. And I only wore your shirt because my shampoo leaked on everything." She motioned to the suitcase. "I had to stick my dress in an empty garbage bag so it wouldn't get ruined by shampoo in the suitcase." At least the janitor had taken pity on her.

She stopped rummaging through her clothes. It was useless. Her hand throbbed, and everything that had happened that afternoon had been a nightmare. She finally looked up at him.

He met her eyes briefly. "Don't go on that dating app anymore."

That was not what she expected to hear. "What?"

"The app. Don't date."

She narrowed her eyes and stood up. "Are you seriously saying that? After the day I've had, and the evening I had, this is the last thing I want to talk about. You have no right to tell me not to date. How's Julie, by the way?"

"Julie is my sister."

"Ha." She sat down again and started repacking her suitcase. She didn't need to have this conversation again. How many times did she have variations of this conversation with Ethan?

"Look, let me explain! Here." He pulled out his phone and held it out to her. She refused to stop packing her suitcase, so he stood up and walked over. He dropped the phone on top of her half-empty suitcase, with a picture showing up. "This is a picture of us from last week. And here's another. And another. Here's one with her son. If you stay tonight, you'll meet them both tomorrow morning when I go there to drop off Boo Boo the Second."

Emily gave him a confused look. Boo Boo the Second?

"The fish. It's for him to replace the one that died last week." He tilted his head to the counter, where the fish swam around inside a glass jar.

Emily shrugged. "These pictures don't prove anything. She doesn't look like you at all."

"I told you. I'm adopted. My parents adopted both of us, separately, a few years apart. We don't share the same blood, but she's my sister."

Emily frowned. All the best cheaters had good excuses. "That's still not proof."

He set his jaw and grabbed the phone. "Fine." He tapped the screen a few times, then held it out to her. She glanced at it, then tentatively took it and held it to her ear.

"Hey, Bill. Did you forget something?" A woman's voice came through clearly.

"Is—is this Julie?" She stared directly at Bill, waiting to see the look on his face when his scheme to make her believe this lie fell apart.

"Yes. Who is this and why do you have Bill's phone?"

"I'm Emily, and—"

"Really? Emily? Is everything ok with Bill? He just left here a little while ago. I'm so sorry I had to interrupt your weekend. After he left this morning, our parents were fine. But Dad went for a walk this evening and got lost. I couldn't find him anywhere. It was a rough night. But everything is better now, and he's safe and back home. I'm really sorry for taking him away from you."

"Your dad got lost?" Emily's mouth hung open in surprise.

"Yes. He has dementia, and, well, I can usually find him on my own but couldn't tonight. I panicked."

"I'm so sorry. I'm glad you found him." She blinked hard.

"Anyway, was there anything you needed? Bill said he'd stop by tomorrow morning to drop of Boo Boo before heading back to the city. I'm really excited to meet you."

"I'm excited to meet you too. I'll have Bill call you in the morning before he heads over."

"Thanks."

Emily ended the call and looked at the phone for a minute. No person could be that good of an actress, especially if they were dating Bill. And she'd called Bill a liar, right to his face. She swallowed hard.

"Bill, I—"

"You believe me now?" His voice lost the angry edge that it had earlier but was still intense.

She nodded. "How did she know who I was?"

"Once we found Dad, I told her about you."

"Oh."

"Emily, I'm crazy for you. I have no right to ask you to be with me and no right to ask you not to date anyone else, but please. Give me some time to see if we can work things out."

"You mean date?" She barely managed to whisper the word *date*. Even though she told Theresa that she was going to start dating again, there was a huge difference between going on a first date with a random guy from a dating app and being in a relationship. Was that even what he was asking? Being in a relationship meant that she'd have to trust him. And how could she trust anyone enough to risk being in a relationship again?

He stood up and started pacing, running his hand through his hair. "I can visit you twice a month, and you can come here the other two weekends each month. No, that won't work. I also need to be on call with the hospital one weekend a month. So three weekends here, one weekend there. Would you be willing to drive here a few times each month?"

"What are you talking about?" She resisted the urge to start pacing on the other side of the room.

"It wouldn't be like that forever. Just a few years. Or you could move to Clareville too."

Emily's eyes widened. "Move to Clareville?" The town sounded familiar. She remembered seeing its name on a map when she looked up directions to the hotel. But how did they go from talking about dating, to a relationship, to moving to a new town? And did he use the word *years*?

"The hospital is small and understaffed. I can talk with

the hospital administration. See if there are any social work positions."

"Bill, what are you talking about?" She tried to hide the panic from her voice.

He stopped pacing and stood in front of her. "You heard Julie. My parents need help. I've already signed a contract with the local hospital and need to move here in a few weeks. But we can make this work."

She opened her mouth to speak, but nothing came out.

"I know it's a lot to ask. Long distance relationships are hard. But I don't want to lose you." His voice cracked as he spoke that last words.

Another wave of fear washed over her. He couldn't actually mean what he was saying. Or maybe he did mean it, right now, in this moment. But a month from now? Or a year from now? When was he going to decide that she wasn't enough for him anymore? When was he going to start cheating on her?

"I can't do a long-distance relationship." She spoke quietly, so quietly that she wasn't sure he heard her.

"We can talk on the phone every night. Text every day. Really get to know each other."

She blinked hard and tried to speak louder. "I can't. I'm sorry, but I can't."

He stopped pacing and sat next to her on the couch. He studied her eyes for a moment. "Am I making this all up? Don't you feel it too?" His words were quieter but intense, like he was trying to hold back.

Emily took a deep breath. All she could smell was him. "Yes. But that doesn't change anything."

"I don't understand. Why not try?"

She shook her head and tried to find the right words. She knew what she wanted to say, needed to say. She didn't want to lie to Bill. "I don't know how to trust you."

He inhaled deeply. "Talk with Michael. Or Julie. Or anyone else who texted me today. They'll all tell you the same thing. I don't cheat. I don't lie. I take care of the people I love. You can trust me."

Her heart fluttered and stalled. "I want to trust you," she whispered. "But I think that part of me is gone."

"If I could stay behind and not move here, I would. I don't care how long it took for you to trust me, but I would do whatever you needed. I want to be the one you call when you need help. I want to be the last person you think of at night when you fall asleep. I want to see you wear my shirt. I'm falling in love with you."

"Bill, I . . ." Emily shook her head and looked away.

"I have to move. I can't back away from my family. But I know . . ." His voice caught and he paused before continuing. "I know that we have something real. Give me a chance to prove it to you."

"I wish I could, Bill." She inhaled deeply and tried to figure out how to say what she needed to say, but the words never came. "I can't."

30

EMILY

Emily finally pulled into her apartment parking lot at noon the next day. She parked the rental car in a spot designated for visitors and gingerly stepped out of the car. Her body ached.

Ashley waved to her from the front door of the apartment building. Three spots away, Theresa got out of her car and walked over to join Emily.

Emily sighed. She'd called Ashley on the way home but completely forgot that Theresa promised to come over and sort through online dating profiles. Well, at least she could talk to both of them at the same time.

Theresa gave Emily a huge hug. "How's your hand? You look tired. I have a few really good guys picked out for you already. And when do you want to go shopping for new dating clothes? Tuesday after work?"

Emily grunted as she lifted her suitcase out of her car with her uninjured hand. "I guess so. I mean, no. I don't know."

Theresa gave her a look that made her feel like a child

who'd misbehaved. "Why are you changing your mind? You sounded completely onboard with this yesterday."

"Let's get inside and I'll tell you and Ashley all the details."

Emily walked toward the entrance to the apartment building where Ashley waited. Theresa followed.

Ashley's friendly smile turned to stone as Emily and Theresa approached. "What's she doing here?" Ashley pointed at Theresa.

Emily turned to the keypad by the door and entered her security code. The door unlocked with a loud click. "Ashley, meet Theresa. She started working in hospice with me a few weeks ago. Theresa, this is my cousin, Ashley."

Ashley spoke in a cold voice. "We've met before. What is she doing here?"

Emily paused halfway through the apartment door. "She's helping me with an online dating profile."

Theresa and Ashley both stared at each other. Emily groaned. She recognized their looks and was tired of drama. "If you both are going to fight, then just get it over with. I'm going upstairs to eat ice cream for lunch."

She pushed through the door and then to the ancient elevator tucked in the corner. Even though it was old and creaked in protest whenever she dared to use it, it didn't require a special key to work. The doors started to close behind her when Ashley and Theresa darted in, neither looking at the other.

Emily stared ahead at the door. "You two ok?"

"Maybe," mumbled Ashley.

Theresa shrugged. "I'm fine."

Emily huffed out a deep breath. She really didn't want to deal with this today.

As soon as she unlocked her apartment door, Ashley went straight to the kitchen. "I dropped off a cheesecake from the restaurant this morning before I ran errands. Do you want that or ice cream?"

Emily didn't even pause to consider. "Both."

She took her suitcase to her room and grabbed two empty laundry baskets from her closet. She quickly dumped all her clothes out of the suitcase, sorted them into the baskets, and carried the larger basket to her washing machine in the cramped bathroom. Once she'd started the load, she went back to her dresser and changed into clean clothes: sweatpants and a shirt that never belonged to Bill and smelled like her laundry detergent, not like him.

Emily walked into the living room and collapsed on the couch. Ashley picked up a bowl from the coffee table and placed it in her hands. Cheesecake topped with ice cream.

"What happened? I need all the details," Ashley asked. Theresa silently ate but looked up.

Emily took a large bite before filling them in on the entire weekend. By the time she finished telling them, she and Ashley were on their second serving of dessert. Theresa was on her third.

"So you just left him after he told you he's falling in love and begged you to date him?" Ashley examined her bowl as she spoke.

Emily just nodded. "Yup. I feel horrible. But what could I do? I got another room, got a rental car this morning, and left."

Ashley sighed. "Why not move to Clareville? He loves you. Plus he's gorgeous. Not as gorgeous as Michael," she quickly interjected, "but it would be like a fairy-tale ending. Girl meets boy, they fall in love, make huge sacrifices to be together, and live happily ever after."

Theresa shook her head. "No. There's no way she can move to Clareville. She'd have to give up her job and everything else. Why should she move away for a guy? There are plenty of other hot guys in the city. Look." She put her bowl down and picked up her phone. She tapped the screen and passed the phone to Ashley. "Here's her dating profile. Look how many guys are already interested!"

Ashley narrowed her eyes. "She's not like you. She's looking for true love, not just any guy."

Theresa grabbed her phone back. "You don't know anything about me. It's Emily's choice, and she said she's not going."

"She shouldn't just turn her back on love. Michael said that Bill has never cheated on anyone. She could do a long-distance relationship, right Em? With a guy who doesn't cheat?" She turned and looked at Emily.

Emily frowned, looking back and forth between Theresa and Ashley, not sure why they were arguing with each other. There must be something she missed between them. "I can't have a long-distance relationship. Ethan cheated on me and we lived just a few blocks apart. How could I trust anyone, even Bill, not to cheat if he lived a few hours away? I can't set myself up for that level of heartbreak again."

Ashley turned to Theresa. "Ethan was her ex-fiancé. You probably don't know that."

Theresa stared back at Ashley. "Of course I know about him. Emily and I are friends. Who do you think took her shopping and helped her get ready for the weekend?"

Ashley ignored her and turned back to Emily. "You have to start trusting people again. Any guy could cheat, no matter how close you live. But Bill wouldn't cheat. He's a good guy. Michael wouldn't be friends with him if he wasn't."

Theresa snorted. "Why would she trust Michael's judgment?"

Ashley narrowed her eyes again at Theresa. "Because he is

a good guy and a good judge of character. He turned you down, right?"

Emily's jaw dropped open. She had never heard Ashley speak like that to anyone. "Ashley!"

Ashley turned back to Emily, eyes on fire. "Do you know that Theresa and I used to run into each other at work? When I worked in housekeeping at the hospital and Theresa was a nurse in the cardiology department with Michael?"

Emily shook her head as she racked her brain for any stories Ashley might have told her about Theresa.

Ashley sighed. "Remember when Michael and I first started dating? I told you about a nurse who was trying to chase after him? It was Theresa. She was jealous."

Theresa let out a loud huff. "I never complained to anyone about you. If anything, you were the one who was jealous. You blamed me for getting you fired, even though I had nothing to do with it."

Ashley narrowed her eyes. "You tried to steal Michael from me."

"First of all, I didn't try to steal him from you. I didn't know you two were serious. Second, of course, I tried to date Michael. Every woman in the hospital did. I'd be stupid not to chase after him. So you can't be angry about that."

Emily looked back and forth as they argued. "Are you two done? I'm trying to figure out what to do about Bill."

Ashley turned back, her eyes wide. "Sorry. You have to date Bill. Either move there, or have a long-distance relationship."

"I can't give up everything for a guy."

"We'll always be your friends, no matter where you live." Ashley glanced sideways at Theresa. "I'll always be your friend."

Theresa shook her head. "You shouldn't have to give up your job to chase after a guy. Look, here's a guy who lives in this city. He's a . . ." she bit her lip and tapped the screen. "It doesn't really matter what he does. He's really cute."

Emily looked over Theresa's shoulder at the screen. "It says he's a bouncer at a local strip club."

Ashley wrinkled her nose. "That's the best you can find for her? Emily, just try a long-distance relationship with Bill."

"Here's another guy. He's a teacher. So he must like kids." Theresa held the phone out so all three of them could see the screen.

Emily looked again and saw a blurry picture of a guy. "He could be a good boyfriend."

Ashley shook her head. "Maybe. But you love Bill. And he loves you."

Emily focused on the picture of the guy on the phone. "I don't know if I love Bill. I like him, but . . . I don't know if I love him."

Ashley flopped back on the couch while Theresa navigated to another guy's dating profile. "This guy's name is Nick. And he likes dogs! Wait, nope. Never mind." She held up a picture of the guy standing with his arm around another woman. "Never date someone who puts a picture of their ex on their dating profile. Trust me on that."

Ashley grunted. "She shouldn't trust you on anything."

Theresa put the phone down and looked at Ashley. "I never try to date a man who's already dating someone. But you can't be mad at me for trying to get his attention before you guys were official. If I had known that you and Michael were actually dating, I wouldn't have flirted with him."

Emily watched as Ashley studied Theresa's face. "Ashley, Theresa's really a great person."

Ashley chewed her lip. "We have different definitions of 'great.' "

Theresa let out a breath of air, almost like a laugh. "Why are you mad? Aren't you a hotshot chef at a restaurant now?"

Ashley blushed. "Not quite, but I'm getting there."

Theresa smirked. "So it all worked out in the end." She turned to Emily. "This will all work out in the end for you too."

Emily gave her a half-smile. Her optimism was encouraging.

Ashley leaned forward. "It will definitely work out. If you don't want to quit your job and find a new one, then just try the long-distance relationship."

"No, try online dating instead." Theresa crossed her arms.

Emily studied her hands for a minute. The swelling had gone down in her hand since the punch yesterday, but her hand still ached a little. "I don't think I can trust him, or anyone, enough to have a long-distance relationship. And I can't quit my job. But . . . what if Bill is the right one for me? What if I mess this up by ending things now?"

Ashley patted her shoulder. "Just try a long-distance relationship. You have to learn to trust guys again."

Theresa shook her head. "If it's meant to be, it will happen. You'll get a sign or something showing you that Bill is the one for you. Look at Ashley. She was destined to be a chef with a hot boyfriend. Even I couldn't stop that."

Ashley shrugged. Emily couldn't tell if she still disliked Theresa or if whatever happened in their past was resolved. After a few awkward seconds, Ashley turned back to Emily. "Let's delete your dating profile. Then you can call Bill and start dating him. A few hours are nothing compared to true love."

"No way," Theresa interjected. "She said she doesn't even know if she's in love, and how can she trust anyone after everything she went through with Ethan? She should definitely meet new guys and go on lots of dates." She turned to face Emily with a wide grin on her face. "We can go on double dates together with the guys we find online!"

Emily cringed and looked back and forth between her two friends.

"Start a long-distance relationship."

"Move on and find a guy here."

Emily frowned. Her head hurt. She just wanted to be alone. "I'm going to take a nap."

31

EMILY

Laughing at work should be illegal. Asking about the weekend should also be illegal. Really, any talk about someone's personal life or dating life—or lakes or boats or hotels —should be outlawed.

Emily thought that one month would be long enough to move on from Bill. She was wrong.

Emily gave Theresa a warning glance as she walked into her office nearly a month after the wedding. "I have a lot of work to do before the staff meeting." She turned back to her computer, opened up a blank document, and started typing random keys. Her monitor had a privacy screen, so it was virtually impossible for any bystanders to see what she was working on.

Theresa sat down anyway, looking comfortable. "There's a new match for you on the app. He looks adorable. He has a dog, plays soccer on the weekends, and likes to hike."

Emily kept typing. "You should ask him out."

She shook her head. "I already have a date for Friday. Why don't you at least give one guy a chance? You spent all that money on the new dress last week. At least give someone a try. If not him, someone else."

"Tell me about your date for Friday." She tried to sound interested. If she had learned anything about Theresa, it was that she could talk for hours if she got excited.

Theresa shrugged. "He's tall, dark, and handsome."

"Sounds perfect."

"Maybe. There's really no way to tell until I meet the guy."

Emily turned back to her computer and started typing again. Her screen displayed a mess of random letters.

"Have you heard from Bill?"

Emily inhaled sharply, then glanced to see if Theresa noticed. She had.

"Why don't you just call him? You said that you wanted to date other guys instead of having a long-distance relationship. But you aren't even trying to date."

"I don't even know what I'd say to him."

"Figure it out when he answers the phone. Or just text him."

"He might not answer. Or he might not feel the same way anymore."

"There's only one way to find out."

Emily pursed her lips and turned back to the computer. "I'm really busy. I have to finish typing this report before I go to the meeting."

Theresa narrowed her eyes, stood up, and walked over to Emily. Before Emily could close the computer window, Theresa's head pressed next to hers so she could see the screen. "You aren't working."

Emily rolled her chair away from Theresa. "Fine. There's no point in thinking of Bill. I missed my chance. And dating someone else feels wrong."

Theresa walked back to her chair. "But he has called, hasn't he?"

She nodded. "A few times. I haven't returned the calls."

Theresa gave her a stern look, then stood up. "You've thrown yourself a pity party for too long. A rebound guy is the perfect solution."

"We need to leave for the staff meeting or we'll be late. Did you get the agenda?"

Theresa shook her head and followed Emily out of her office and down the hall. "No. Honestly, even if I had, I never look at it until I get there. Do you think there will be donuts?"

"Yes. I brought them this week."

Theresa stopped and gave her a quick hug. "You are the best. Really. As a thank you, I'm going to set you up on your date tomorrow night. Nothing fancy, just dinner with Neil. He's my favorite of all your matches so far. I'll email him the details, and you don't have to do anything except show up and have a good time."

Theresa filled her in on all the details of Neil's profile as they walked into the conference room and helped themselves to the donuts. As more people shuffled into the room, Theresa shifted to greeting their other co-workers. For someone who hated working in the hospice unit just weeks ago, Theresa had managed to make friends with nearly the entire team in record time.

Emily tried to pay attention to the meeting. Her boss, Susan, sat at the front of the room, and was going over another presentation slide projected onto a large screen. Emily tried to look interested as Susan's monotonous voice filled the room. That task was hard enough on a good day, but today, it was impossible, even with the energy boost from the sugar in the donuts.

Why couldn't she find the energy to go on a date with one of her matches? Bill couldn't be the only man in the state who made her feel sparks. He argued with her at the coffee shop, in her parking lot, at the hotel, but he also made her feel safe and secure. Like he could read into her soul.

How could she find a man like that based on an online dating profile?

A collective groan came from the table. Emily glanced up from her doodle to see what caused the reaction. Susan stood in front of a familiar presentation slide.

Susan droned on over the continued groans and complaints. "We need to work together as a team. Remember, the patients come first. Until we hire a social work replacement for the northern region, everyone needs to pitch in. I've set up week-long rotations for the social workers for the next three months. Rhonda, you'll start first. Claire, you'll take over the second week. Emily—" Susan stopped talking as the seven other social workers at the table continued to grumble.

Emily watched but didn't join in with her own complaints. No one wanted to hear about how all the good men were already taken or lived too far away.

Susan's face grew red, and she spoke louder than usual. "Listen, I didn't want to create this schedule. I've been telling everyone for weeks that we'd have to start traveling there to fill in for the person who quit. You'll get a small bonus for the weeks you go, but I can't do anything else. Henrietta is supposed to be beautiful. Near some lakes, near the woods, no traffic problems."

The other social workers in the room continued to grumble. Emily reached for another donut but stopped when she felt a sharp pain on her shin.

"Ouch, Theresa, what's wrong? One extra donut won't hurt anybody. There's still plenty left."

Theresa nudged her excitedly. "What's wrong with you?" she whispered.

"Nothing. I want a donut. I'm having a hard week. Leave me alone."

Theresa rolled her eyes dramatically. "I don't care about the donut. Take them all. But why are you just letting everyone else complain about going to Henrietta?"

She hovered her hand over a chocolate donut but then moved to the apple fritter. "What should I do instead? Volunteer to go every week myself?"

"Yes!"

Emily grabbed the donut and turned to Theresa. "What are you talking about? First, you want me to go on blind dates with half of the city. Now you are telling me to move to Henrietta. I don't even know where that is." She took a large bite of the donut.

Theresa pushed her phone over to Emily with a map displayed on the screen. Henrietta was ten minutes away from Clareville. They were practically the same town.

The bite of donut in her mouth became dry and she struggled to swallow. If she volunteered for the social work position in Henrietta, she could be with Bill. See his smile every day. Feel his strong arms wrap around her. Hold his hand as they walked down the street together. She'd have the chance to try at a real relationship again.

A smaller voice crept up from the back of her head. Moving to Henrietta could make more problems. There'd been no communication between her and Bill for weeks. He could have moved on. A guy like him could have any woman he wanted. Why would he possibly want her anymore, after she turned him down? And moving to Henrietta would mean that she was ready for a relationship again. Ready to trust another man with her heart and believe that he could be faithful.

She looked to Theresa. "What should I do?"

Theresa stood up. "Emily will go!"

Susan and everyone else stopped what they were doing and turned to look at her.

Emily froze. The only sound in the room was her heart thumping wildly in her chest. There might never be another chance like this.

"I'll go. I'll go to Henrietta every week. I'll fill in there so no one else has to go." Emily tried to ignore the fear behind her words as she spoke. But even as she spoke, hope began to take over. She wanted this chance. More than she realized moments ago.

Susan frowned. "I already made up the schedule."

"Yes, I know that, but no one else wants to go."

She crossed her arms. "Why didn't you say something last week?"

Emily's face grew warm again. She looked around the room. "I changed my mind."

"Why? Is it the bonus? Because there might be other people in the room who want the bonus money too." A few people started to whisper again.

No one but Theresa could know the truth of why she needed. "I just thought . . . well . . ."

"Susan, if Emily wants to go, let her." Beth gave Emily an encouraging smile. Soon, others joined in.

Susan pressed her lips together. "It would make the schedule easier to manage. Alright, let's have a show of hands. All social workers in favor of Emily taking over the Henrietta vacancy until a permanent replacement is hired, raise your hand."

Emily looked around the room at all the raised hands. She nudged Theresa. "I don't think you're allowed to vote. You're a nurse and can't fill in for this position."

Theresa shrugged and raised her other hand.

"Emily, congratulations, you'll start in Henrietta on Monday."

32

EMILY

Emily paced up Main Street in Clareville. Again. The small coffee shop closed an hour ago, and the owner of the bookstore was getting ready to do the same.

The thought of spending another day wandering the quiet streets of this small town, hoping to run into Bill, did not sound appealing.

If she were Bill, she'd have let someone know where she was and where she was moving to. It was like he had vanished off the face of the earth. He hadn't answered her calls earlier today, he hadn't answered Michael's call, and no one knew his new address.

Of all her bad ideas, this had to be the worst. Who impulsively agreed to move hours away to chase a man she turned down weeks ago?

Not to mention that she had no idea what to say to Bill if she ever found him.

A scent of cooking spices caught her attention. She looked across the street at the largest restaurant in this section of town. Her stomach grumbled, sending her the message.

As she crossed the street, she looked closely at the surrounding cars. None belonged to Bill.

She opened the door to the restaurant and inhaled deeply. The hostess glanced at her with a bored expression. "Do you have a reservation?"

"No, I don't." She looked around the room but didn't see Bill at any of the closest tables.

"How many are in your party?"

"One. Just me." Unless Bill miraculously walked through that door in the next thirty seconds.

"I'll see what I can do." The hostess walked away while Emily took a few cautious steps into the dining area.

If Bill were here, he'd definitely try to sit at a table in the back, in a secluded corner. But he'd also want to have a view of the door, which meant she might be able to see him if he was actually here. She glanced at one area of the room but realized he wouldn't want to sit in that section. It was too close to the kitchen door, which meant an ever-revolving rotation of people walking by. Another section was near the entrance to the restrooms, so he probably wouldn't want to sit there. She scanned the tables anyway, with no luck. The next section seemed better. There was a table in a corner, far away from the windows and entrances. If he came to the restaurant, he'd probably want to sit there. But a large group of people sat at that table. He wasn't there.

The hostess came back and directed Emily to follow her to a small table with two place settings. Heat rose in her cheeks as the hostess removed the second place setting, letting everyone in the restaurant know that she was alone.

Someone should really start a restaurant designed specifically for solo diners so they wouldn't have to sit in a crowded restaurant full of happy couples and families.

The menu looked decent, maybe even appealing if she was in a different mood. When the server appeared moments later, she picked something out without really caring what it was and asked the server to rush her order. The sooner she got out of the restaurant, the sooner she could continue her search.

She started typing a text to Ashley when someone sat down at her table. Her heart skipped a beat as she looked up.

A man sat there, beaming at her. "Well, here I am. What are your other two wishes?"

She stared back at him. "What?"

He shifted arrogantly and reached out his hand. "I'm Dave."

"Are you here to meet someone? I don't think I'm the person you're looking for." The poor guy was probably trying out online dating. She twisted in her seat and looked behind her again. There were no other tables with just one person.

"I've found who I'm looking for."

Emily's stomach sank as she realized what this guy was doing. "I'm not interested."

"That's because you don't know me. Yet."

"I don't need to know you. I'm not here to find a guy." She cringed as she realized what she said. She was definitely there to find a guy. Just not Dave.

"Are you new in town? I don't recognize you."

She looked at him directly. If he recognized most people in town, then maybe he knew Bill. "Do you know anyone named Bill?"

He shifted in his chair, no longer trying to charm her. "Does Bill have a last name?"

"Dunham. Bill Dunham."

"Nope."

She chewed her lip. "What about Julie Dunham?"

"I know her."

"Good. Can you tell me her number? Or her address?"

She tried not to be annoyed that he didn't offer up the fact that he knew anyone with that last name. It wasn't like it was very common.

He leaned forward and narrowed his eyes. "Are you a detective or something? Or a private investigator? Police?"

"No. Just trying to find my friend." She tried to sound casual.

The lopsided grin appeared on his face again. "Then I have to arrest you for stealing."

Emily's jaw dropped open. "What? Arrest me? Are you a cop or something? I didn't do anything wrong." Except try to stalk a man for the past three hours. She pushed her chair back from the table.

He held out his hands. "Wait, stop. It was just a pickup line. If I was a cop, I would arrest you for stealing my breath. Get it?" He looked at her expectantly.

"Do those lines ever work?" If this was what getting back into the dating game would involve, count her out.

He shook his head. "Not really. But maybe one day." He didn't look disappointed.

"Look, can I just have Julie's phone number?"

"How about I get your number and pass it along to Julie?"

Emily studied his face intently. "How do I know you'll pass it along to Julie and that this isn't another pickup attempt?"

"You won't know unless you try."

33

EMILY

The Henrietta Clinic was a two-story building that looked like a relic from the last century. The large window in her office, overlooking the woods, and the coffee shop in the lobby were Emily's saving grace.

Her third cup of coffee grew cold on her desk by late afternoon on Monday. Patients filled her schedule for tomorrow, and she still needed to figure out how to work the department's scanner. It looked like the last social worker's record-keeping system had also belonged in the last century.

Which meant Emily was going to spend a long night at the office trying to prepare for tomorrow.

It also meant that her search for Bill had officially failed.

Either Dave didn't hold up his end of the bargain after she cautiously gave him her phone number, or Julie decided not to pass along her message to Bill.

Or, Bill decided she wasn't worth chasing any longer. She had refused to call him back for the past month, after all.

A noise in the hallway drew her attention. She looked across her desk to her open office door.

"Nice meeting you today, Emily. See you tomorrow." The unit administrator walked past Emily's office on her way out for the day.

"Bye." Emily let her voice trail off and looked at the clock again.

There had to be a better way to locate Bill. Michael must have heard from him by now, which meant that Bill probably wanted nothing to do with her anymore.

She moved here for nothing.

Work kept her busy for the next hour as she tried to decipher the handwritten notes from the previous social worker. Her first client tomorrow couldn't actually be eighty eleven years old. And the one after that couldn't actually have three arms—or heads.

She would give herself a week to settle in here. One week. After that, she'd call Susan and beg if she had to, to return to her old position.

A loud, rumbling noise came from her stomach. Food would make this evening better. Emily grabbed her purse, doubtful that any of the small restaurants she passed on her way through town this morning would deliver to the hospital. Besides, she could use a short walk.

Emily walked past the ancient elevator to the stairway that led to the main entrance. As she rounded the corner and could see the glass doors, she saw movement in the parking lot.

Her eyes must have been playing tricks on her because she could have sworn that the car that pulled into the lot looked like Bill's.

The car pulled into the closest parking space, directly in front of the main glass doors.

Now she knew her eyes were definitely playing tricks on her and that she probably needed something to eat more than ever since she was seeing something that couldn't be possible. She rubbed her eyes and looked again.

Bill stepped out of the driver's seat of his car.

Without meaning to, Emily dashed out the front entrance to the building, the cool breeze catching her off-guard and blowing her hair around her shoulders. She shivered and ran to his car.

"Emily." With one quick movement, Bill slid his suit jacket off his shoulders and placed it around Emily, letting his hands linger on her shoulders.

"How did you—?" The words weren't coming out of her mouth, no matter how hard she tried. She still couldn't believe that he was in front of her.

"Julie texted me last night. She said that you were looking for me. Or that Dave said you were looking for me. How do you know Dave?"

"You didn't answer my calls this weekend."

He looked down for a moment like he was ashamed. "I needed to clear my head. The last few weeks have been long."

"Are your parents ok?" Emily tried not to think of the possibility that his parents' health had declined any further.

"They're ok. Well, not exactly ok, but they aren't doing any worse than usual. Julie and I are working to find more reliable help during the week. But we might need to move Dad somewhere safer in the next few months." His eyes grew distant as he spoke.

She waited a minute until he looked back at her, no longer lost in his thoughts. She licked her lips and inhaled deeply. The scent from his jacket gave her courage.

"I started a new position." She pointed over her shoulder at the building behind them as if he hadn't driven here and watched her leave the building moments earlier.

He touched the employee ID badge clipped onto her shirt. "Says temporary social worker?"

"The previous hospice social worker retired, and they still can't find a new person to take over. So I'm filling in for the next three months. After that, I could request to stay here permanently." She broke eye contact as she said the last words.

"Is that what you really want?" Doubt laced his words.

"Is this what you want?" She threw the question back in his face, trying to ignore the knots in her stomach.

He remained silent for a minute. "I can't ask you to move here."

"I already did."

"I can't expect you to give up your life, everything you had, to move here for me. I can't ask you to do that."

"I never said I was moving here for you."

Bill's eyes flared at those words, giving Emily the response she expected. "What do you mean? I told you last month how I feel. I love you, and nothing's changed my feelings for you. If you aren't here because you have feelings for me, then why are you here?"

"I moved here for me. Me." She pointed at her chest. "I want to be selfish. I want to choose the man I spend time with. I choose where I live and where I work. And I'm choosing this job, in this town, and I'm asking you to be my boyfriend again. I'm choosing to trust you, because I love you too." The words tumbled out, leaving her out of breath.

He closed the distance between them and wrapped his hands around the opening of his jacket that was still draped over her shoulders. The pressure from his hands drew her closer to his chest. She angled her head to look up at him.

"Is this what you really want?"

She didn't hesitate. "More than anything."

He released his hold on her arms and stepped back, putting up a hand between them to stop her. "I have a few conditions."

Her mouth dropped open. Wasn't this the time that he was supposed to kiss her senseless?

"You delete the dating app on your phone."

She rolled her eyes. "Already done."

"I get to take you on a date every Friday. I pay."

"Every Friday, fine. We split the bill," she countered.

He gave the first hint of a real smile, with the crooked lip that turned up higher on the right side. "We get together every Saturday and Sunday, except when I'm helping my parents."

She gave him a firm look. "We get together every Saturday and Sunday. I'll spend time with your parents and help when needed." He raised an eyebrow. "They are important to you, so they are important to me."

He nodded briefly. "Do you have any conditions?"

"You need to give me one of your t-shirts."

"Why?"

"To sleep in."

He nodded. "I'll give you two. Anything else?"

"No. You?"

"I have one last condition."

"What?" Whatever it was, her answer would be yes.

"Kiss me."

Emily reached up on her tiptoes to meet Bill's lips. He pressed his mouth against hers in a move that was better than she remembered. She had tried her best to forget the feeling of his mouth pressed against his since they'd last said goodbye. She'd spent countless hours, alone at night, trying to think of anything except the feel of the stubble from his five o'clock shadow rubbing against her cheek. She'd torn herself away from the men's section of the shampoo aisle of the grocery store, too tempted to smell each bottle until she found one that smelled like the kind of shampoo he used.

And now that his lips were finally pressed to hers, and his arms pressing her body even closer to his, he kissed her like he was never going to stop.

And that was fine with her.

EPILOGUE

After several hours of gourmet food at Emily and Bill's going-away party, the crowd in the private dining room of *Harvest House* was starting to thin out. The first couple left about five minutes ago, and another couple looked like they were getting ready to leave. The desert dishes had already been cleared. Theresa estimated that she could probably sneak away within the next fifteen minutes without anyone noticing.

Not that there was anyone here that she wanted to be noticed by. Emily invited her to the dinner a week ago. Almost everyone they worked with at the hospice department in the hospital was there, along with too many of Emily's family members to count. Emily had promised that Bill had invited his former coworkers from his hospital. Sure enough Theresa met several doctors and surgeons, all of whom looked rich but none of whom were single.

If it weren't for the fact that Emily was one of her only friends, she would have been mad that she wasted a perfectly good night for dating on attending a dinner at a fancy restaurant filled with couples. Being the only single person in a room was brutal.

But since Emily had been nicer to her than almost anyone, she put on a large smile and pretended like she wasn't jealous that everyone in the room had someone to depend on. Either a family member or partner who was sitting by their side.

"Ashely, the chocolate soufflé was incredible. Did you help make that?" Theresa spoke to the woman sitting across from her at the small table. Emily must have thought she was being kind by placing Theresa at the same table as Ashley, Michael, and another couple who Theresa'd never met before, but weren't particularly talkative.

A muscle in Ashley's jaw twitched. "No, I usually work on the seafood station. Plus, I'm not working tonight."

"Right." Theresa's face grew red. Of course Ashley wouldn't have made the dessert, since she wasn't working in the *Harvest House* kitchen tonight. "Well, the restaurant looks like a nicer place to work than the cleaning department at the hospital."

A scowl formed over Ashley's face and Theresa regretted her words. Why did she always do that? She could never say the right thing. She just meant to compliment the restaurant, not insult Ashley. Ashley used to work at the same hospital as Theresa, cleaning floors, but got fired.

Michael leaned over to whisper something in Ashley's ear, and Theresa looked away. She didn't care that she and Ashley had fought for Michael's attention at the same time. There were lots of other rich men in the city. Ashley could have him. She just hated that Michael accused her of getting Ashley fired due to jealousy.

It wasn't jealousy. She could deal with jealousy.

And she didn't know Ashley would get fired if she filed a

complaint against her and Michael. But Ashley and Michael had fought and then kissed in the stairway at work one evening, blocking her path out of the hospital. By the time she'd made it to the parking lot using a different exit, it was too late. Anyone in her situation would have complained about that.

Michael stood up and held his hand out to Ashley. They were getting ready to leave. Theresa swallowed hard, knowing that this could be her last chance to ask Ashley the question that had been at the back of her mind all night.

"Ashley?"

Michael and Ashley froze and stared at her.

"I was wondering, I mean, I don't know if you know or not." Theresa took a deep breath and urged herself to continue. "What I wanted to know is, what does the restaurant do with all their leftover food each night?"

Michael and Ashley looked at her like she had two heads. She tried to act like it didn't bother her.

Ashley stood up next to Michael. "I don't know. Compost it, I guess."

Michael held up a hand to wave goodbye, and Ashley led him away from their table.

She missed her chance. She waited too long, and missed her chance to find out if the restaurant was willing to donate any of their leftover food at the end of each day to the local soup kitchen.

The other couple seated at the table were involved in their own conversation. Theresa was officially the third wheel at the table.

She stood up and scanned the room until she saw Emily and Bill chatting with someone in the corner of the room. This was it, her last chance to say goodbye to Emily. Even though she and Bill acted like they were meant for each other, she never should have encouraged Emily to move away. But wasn't that what people always did? Leave?

"Emily, thanks for inviting me. I had an amazing time." Theresa mustered up as much enthusiasm in her voice as she could manage, and hoped her smile looked genuine.

Emily turned and surprised her with a warm hug. "I'm going to miss you so much."

Theresa tried not to stiffen in response to Emily's words. "You'll be too busy with your job and dating Bill. You won't have time to miss me."

"I'll still be here once a month for department meetings, and we can text all the time."

Theresa pulled back and looked at Emily's face. She looked like she meant it. "That would be great."

"Don't act surprised. We're friends, and we'll stay friends."

Theresa swallowed the lump that formed in her throat.

"And don't forget, I promised I'd help you with online dating. We're going to find the perfect guy for you."

Theresa tried not to say something to break Emily's enthusiasm. She didn't want the perfect guy.

She needed a rich guy.

NEWSLETTER/ALSO BY LACEY BOLT

NEWSLETTER SIGN UP

Curious what Dr. Tobers wrote in his journal about Ashley? Sign up for my newsletter and you will get a free copy of the short story Michael Tobers, M.D. Journal for free! Sign up for the newsletter at laceybolt.com/fake_boyfriend.

ALSO BY LACEY BOLT

Don't Fall for the Doctor

Don't Fall for the Fake Boyfriend

Printed in Great Britain
by Amazon

44566409R00139